MISTY TREASURE

A MISTY POINT MYSTERY

LINDA RAWLINS

MISTY TREASURE

Misty Treasure
A Misty Point Mystery

By
Linda Rawlins

E-Book: 978-0-9914230-9-5
Paperback: 978-0-9600549-9-2

Discover other titles by Linda Rawlins at
www.lindarawlins.com

This book is a work of fiction. Names, characters, places, and incidents either are the product of the author's imagination or are used fictitiously. Any resemblance to actual persons, living or dead, business establishments, events, or locales is entirely coincidental.

ACKNOWLEDGMENTS

I want to thank everyone for their dedication to Misty Treasure. It's always a journey to complete a book and I appreciate the efforts of all who have traveled this journey with me.

To the staff of Riverbench Publishing for a great job and all the support!

My first circle of readers – Joyce, Joe, Sandy, Lorraine, Anita, Krista and of course, Matt! You are the best treasures ever.

My many readers, librarians, booksellers and friends - your enthusiasm and encouragement inspire me daily. Thank you for reading and sharing my stories. I always love hearing from you.

Matthew 6:21

For where your heart is, there your treasure will be also.

To

My Grandchildren

My Greatest Treasures

CHAPTER 1

"What's wrong?" Megan asked as she watched the man before her.

He stood up and scratched his silver head of hair. "I think we have a problem."

"Already? We haven't even started."

"Something's off with the blueprints." Placing a hand on the cherrywood table, he rubbed his grizzled chin.

"Can you check again? Maybe you missed something."

Nathan Graham smiled as he looked at Megan. His expression was that of an adult being tolerant of a child's ignorant remarks. "I assure you I didn't miss anything, and I'll confirm everything before I release my report."

Megan took a deep breath. "I wish something went smoothly for once. What seems to be the problem?"

"The measurements are off." He tapped the paper and looked up. "According to the measurements, this room should be ten feet longer than it is."

Megan looked around the beautiful cherrywood library. The walls were lined with bookcases which held an extraordinary collection of books amassed over the last hundred years. Some were rare first editions brought back from Europe by her great-grandfather, John Stanford. Others were favorite reads. Regardless of value, most were beloved and cherished.

One wall of the library boasted large windows with a beautiful view of the ocean. Waves curled to the shore while seagulls circled above. Sunlight glittered off the water like diamonds dancing in the surf.

When the library was empty, heavy damask curtains protected the books from strong sunlight. A velvet covered reading nook, topped by a mound of pillows, sat under one of the large windows. Megan always considered it the perfect place to rest with a good book when it was raining.

A large desk sat at the end of the library as well as a heavy cherry-wood table surrounded by six chairs. Grandmother Rose used to help Megan with her homework at the table. The library was the room Grandmother Rose loved so much and the room where all official family business was conducted such as meetings and reading of wills.

Snapping back to attention, Megan said, "This room is as I remember it from my childhood."

"I'm sure it is. These plans are old," Nathan said as he tapped the prints with the back of two fingers. "Over a hundred years old to be exact. I was able to get a copy from your attorney, Teddy. As far as I know, these are the original plans from the estate historical records. I have no idea how much reconstruction was done over the last hundred years, but I can tell you these measurements do not match this room." Nathan scanned the walls and bookcases once again, frowned and shook his head. "There are times when construction doesn't match blueprints for a variety of reasons, but I'm not sure if the original build differed or if the plans were modified."

"There's been no reconstruction in the last thirty years," Megan said as she looked at the architect. "Does it matter?" She shrugged her shoulders for emphasis.

He stared at her for a moment before he spoke. "Yes, it does matter. Especially when you're planning on reconstructing a home.

You have to make sure your support structures are stable." Nathan spoke to her in the simplest way possible.

Insulted, Megan frowned. "Thank you, Mr. Graham. I truly understand the concept, but how do we know what they did one hundred years ago? There have been no changes in this room since I was a child and the house has stood its own against time and some very strong storms."

Nathan smiled. "I think the fact the house sits on a hill helped save it from flooding during Hurricane Sandy."

"Yes, but you understand what I mean."

Nathan walked the room, looked at the walls and shrewdly made calculations in his head while Megan watched him work. They had been scheduled to meet last December, but an unexpected life agenda, including violence in the local animal shelter, had forced the appointment to be postponed until Spring. It was now May. The summer was approaching and with it many happy expectations of those who live near the beach. Megan wanted the paperwork processed so construction could start in the fall. She didn't want to rebuild during the summer and interfere with tourists or homeowners. The last thing she needed was to give Mayor Andrew Davenport a reason to threaten her again.

Megan stopped her reverie and looked up when Nathan called out to her. "Please tell me what you know about the history of Misty Manor."

"Okay, but I can only tell you what I've been told over the years."

"Good enough, but before you start, do you have a public historical archive of Misty Manor or Misty Point somewhere? Perhaps the library or town hall?"

Megan paused for a moment. "Not that I know of, but I'll ask Teddy. I believe he has the most knowledge of the house."

Theodore Harrison Carter, known as Teddy, was the estate attorney for Misty Manor. He had been friends with Rose Stanford, Megan's grandmother, and helped managed the estate until Rose's death upon which the bulk of the estate was inherited by Megan, who had returned to New Jersey to take care of her grandmother in her final days.

Rose had been a powerful, wealthy woman who ran many philanthropic committees and strove to help everyone she could with her blessings. Upon Rose's death, Megan agreed to take over her position as board chair for the Stanford Grants as well as the estate. Megan was learning everything she could about Misty Manor and the town of Misty Point from Teddy. Jonathan Brandon Carter, Teddy's very available son, was also learning so he could continue Teddy's work when he retired. Megan's cop boyfriend, Nick Taylor, had other ideas.

"I'd suggest starting an archive if one doesn't exist."

Megan shook her head. "I'm sorry, I got lost in my thoughts for a moment. What did you say?"

Nathan took a deep breath and restarted. "I'd like you to tell me what you know about Misty Manor, but I was suggesting you start a public historical archive about the town and specifically Misty Manor. This house is a gorgeous Grand Victorian, over a hundred years old, which must have a lot of rich memories and perspective about the last century on the Jersey Coast."

"I'm sure it does," Megan said. "My grandmother, Rose, left some information for me. I haven't had time to digest it all, but I plan to start as soon as possible. I'm learning a lot from Teddy, but I don't think any private information has been made public at this point."

"Just the historical perspective," Nathan suggested. "Better the information come from you than misinformation from public records."

"Sounds logical," Megan said as she nodded.

Nathan pulled out a chair and sat down. Grabbing a yellow legal pad and a pen, he looked at Megan. "Okay, tell me what you know about the history of this place."

Megan paused for a moment to collect her thoughts. "I grew up here, but kids don't pay attention to certain things. What I do know is that my great-grandfather, John Stanford, was a sea captain. He journeyed to Europe and other places during the early 1900's. In 1910, he was given a large amount of undeveloped property on the coast of

New Jersey, as a gift for completing a voyage to Europe for a very rich man. He then married my great-grandmother, Mary Stanford, and as a wedding gift, he had Misty Manor, this beautiful Grand Victorian, built for her.

"The house was very impressive for that time, with three floors, a walk-in attic and widow's walk on top. There were many rooms in the house, with bedrooms on both the second and third floor which is why a lot of famous, important guests stayed here in the early 1900's."

Megan paused and smiled for a moment.

"Don't stop now," Nathan said as he tapped his pen on the pad. "Not only is this necessary, but it's also fascinating. There should be a feature about the Stanford family in the local newspaper. Please tell me your grandmother left you a guest book with the names of the people who stayed here."

Megan laughed. "I remember being told they had grand parties. My great-grandparents had an excellent cook who made delicious meals. There were parlor games, after dinner cognac and cigars for the men, as well as aperitifs for the women. It was quite the destination."

"Fascinating," Nathan encouraged her.

"There was a railroad stop not too far away from the house. Guests would travel to the shore by train and then take a horse-drawn carriage to the house."

"You don't see that anymore," Nathan observed dryly.

"That's for sure. Anyway, my grandfather built the town of Misty Point around the estate of Misty Manor, and over the years the town has grown and prospered."

"I'm sure there are public records we can find."

"Yes, I imagine there are," Megan agreed. "Anyway, John and Mary had a son named George, who was my grandfather. I believe he was born in 1920. He eventually married my grandmother, Rose, in 1945 and they lived here with John and Mary. By then, my great-grandparents were getting up in years; there were new methods of travel as well as new destinations, so the parties and guests at Misty Manor had died off."

"My father, Dean, was born in 1950, but when he was young, my grandfather, George, suddenly disappeared. Rose and Dean were visiting her family, but when they returned, George was gone. The mystery wasn't solved until last year, right before Rose passed away."

"I heard about that," Nathan said. "Very interesting."

"To be honest, I don't think Rose planned to leave this earth until she found George and thankfully, she finally did. It was quite a mystery until we solved it. Anyway, Rose and my father lived with John and Mary until my great-grandparents passed away. The house was willed to George and Rose, in hopes he would return, but at some point, George was legally declared dead, so the entire estate went to Rose and stayed within the extended family.

"They must have truly loved her because she was not of the bloodline. That's a bit unusual," Nathan pointed out.

"Rose was a wonderful woman," Megan said with a sad smile. "She had it tough, raising a son by herself in an isolated area. My father was always a problem. My great-grandparents recognized that and thought their legacy was safer with Rose."

"So, who owns the estate now?" Nathan asked and watched her for an answer.

Megan was quiet for a moment. "I do."

"That makes everything simple. I want to make sure all changes are legal and stay within the original vision of the estate. Sometimes, change is more complicated with a large group."

Megan nodded and folded her hands in front of her. "I appreciate that, and I'm sure Teddy will go over all the legalities necessary for reconstruction, but I am now the legal owner of Misty Manor and therefore, can do what I please."

"That's the next thing we need to discuss. I'd like to know what your goals are. I want to envision what you see in your mind, so I know we're on the same page."

Nathan waited patiently for Megan to answer.

"In a nutshell, I'd like to modernize the working parts of the home. The kitchen needs attention as well as the bathrooms. On the other hand, I want to keep the original charm and beauty of Misty Manor."

"The grand staircase is gorgeous," Nathan said. "You'll not find many like that anymore, especially ones that climb three flights with spacious landings in between."

Megan laughed. "I used to run up and down all three flights as well as back and forth on the landings when I was small."

Nathan chuckled as she spoke.

"I even tried to slide down the banisters but started from the third floor. Rose would worry I'd fall and break my neck."

"Thankfully, that didn't happen," Nathan said. They both looked up when the doorbell rang. "Don't tell me you still have the original doorbell?"

"It's been that way for the last thirty years," Megan said. "Beyond that, I wouldn't know. Please excuse me. I need to get the door."

"That's fine. I want a few minutes to remeasure this room. When you come back, we can continue to go over plans."

"Of course," Megan said as she moved her chair and stood up.

CHAPTER 2

*M*egan left Nathan in the library and walked to the foyer where her dog, Dudley, greeted her. Dudley moved in last December when the local animal shelter was left in crisis after someone shot the veterinarian. A Stanford Grant funded the Hand in Paws animal shelter. As a result, Megan helped the police find the shooter and kept one of her grandmother's favorite charitable causes alive. Some of the animals were fostered until help could arrive. Against her judgment, Megan looked after a Boxer named Dudley and his companion, a young, grey striped kitty named Smokey. Weeks later, Megan decided to formally adopt both pets after Dudley risked his life defending hers.

Megan knelt, rubbed Dudley's head as he nuzzled her neck and then stood and turned toward the front door. Glancing through the window pane, she was surprised to see her boyfriend, Nick Taylor, standing on the porch. She opened the door and smiled her welcome.

"Nick, I wasn't expecting you," Megan said as she stepped forward to hug him. Before they could embrace, Dudley rushed forward and jumped up to greet Nick. "Someone's very happy to see you."

Nick smiled as he rubbed the dog behind the ears. "What a good boy."

Megan cleared her throat as she crossed her arms and posed. "Okay, I'm next."

Nick let Dudley drop to the floor and stepped forward to pull Megan into his arms. He kissed her gently on the lips and mussed her hair.

"What are you up to?" Nick asked as he stepped back.

"The architect, Nathan Graham, is here in the library," Megan said as she pointed. "We're going over the original blueprints for Misty Manor, so I can modernize some of the rooms, but as expected, there's already a problem."

"What kind of problem?"

"He says the measurements are off. The original plans indicate the library should be ten feet longer than it actually is."

"That's weird, but construction methods were completely different when Misty Manor was built."

"Yeah, that's what he said. Why don't you come to the library and meet him?"

"I'd like that. I almost studied to be an architect. Blueprints can be fascinating."

"If you say so," Megan said as she walked toward the library. Dudley followed behind. He was allowed to come into the room but not on the furniture as Megan wanted to preserve everything as long as possible. Weeks ago, Megan had placed a soft dog bed near the fireplace for him to enjoy. Dudley immediately made himself comfortable and with an anxious sigh placed his head on the pillow.

Nathan looked up when the pair entered and waited until they made their way to the table.

"Nick Taylor," Nick said as he extended his hand.

"Nathan Graham. Nice to meet you." The men shook hands and got down to business.

"I hope you don't mind, but Nick would like to glance at the blueprints. At one time he had an interest in becoming an architect." Megan smiled as she looked at the two men.

"Not at all," Nathan said. "The more, the merrier. Maybe he'll be able to help us figure this out." Nathan turned to Nick. "I'm looking at the measurements for the library. I'll grant you the house is over one hundred years old and who knows how closely they followed blueprints back then, but they don't match. Megan said there hadn't been any changes since she was a child so I'm going to assume any changes made, were years ago."

"Can I take a peek?" Nick asked looking past Nathan's shoulder.

"Sure thing." Nathan pushed the blueprints toward Nick and stepped aside.

"I haven't looked at blueprints in a while, but I've always enjoyed trying to visualize a completed project." Nick pulled the papers toward him. He studied the pages, then stood up and looked around the room before bending forward and examining the blueprints again. He measured with his fingers, marking off distance and direction.

"What are you seeing?" Nathan asked with curiosity.

"I'm not positive, but it looks like the changes are at the end of the room, somewhere around the fireplace."

"Exactly what I saw," Nathan said, excitedly. "According to those prints, the fireplace is ten feet forward of where it was supposed to be. So, the obvious question is…"

"What's on the other side of that wall?" Nick and Megan voiced together.

Nathan turned and looked at her with raised eyebrows. "You know the house better than anyone else. If you left the library, walked down the foyer and turned left, what would you find?"

Megan thought for a moment. "I know I'm not as quick as you two with the room visualization, but here goes. When you walk through the front door, you come into a large foyer.

To the right is the living room and beyond that is the solarium. To the left is the library. Straight ahead is the grand staircase which leads up to the landing on the next floor. When you go around the staircase, you walk down the hall. The kitchen is on the right. On the left is my grandmother's office. Beyond that is the entrance to the formal dining room."

"Do the dimensions make sense?" Nathan asked as he questioned her. "Close your eyes and think about each room. Does the combined dimension equal all that space?"

Megan shook her head. "I'm not sure. There could be extra space there."

They looked up to see Nick examining the fireplace. He was bending forward, peering at the mantel, pushing on bricks and picking up each item on display. Megan and Nathan walked toward him to watch him search.

"I know what you're doing, but I'd rather you say it," Megan said as she stood next to Nick.

"It's not uncommon there would be a secret passage or room, especially in a house built in the early 1900's," Nick said with a shrug.

"Where would something like that lead to?" Megan asked.

Nathan nodded. "A tunnel to the beach is a possibility. It would be difficult to maintain due to sand, but it's happened, or it could be as simple as a neatly hidden storage space."

Megan stepped back and watched as both men examined the fireplace with interest. She turned to her right and scanned the titles on the nearest bookshelves. Many were original, valuable books. One by one, Megan picked up each book, opened the front cover, examined the copyright and publisher and placed it back on the shelf.

Megan had hired an appraiser who indicated the books were worth a lot of money, but Megan hadn't had a chance to follow up. She made a mental note to make cataloging the books a priority. She wanted to do what was necessary to preserve them.

Reaching the last book, she pulled it off the shelf. It was an original copy of *Treasure Island*, first published in book form in November 1883 by Cassell & Co. She carefully opened the book cover which was now almost 135 years old. Despite the age, it looked to be in pretty good condition.

Nervous that her hands were dirty, she tried to place the book back on the shelf but had difficulty fitting it in. She gently placed the book on the nearby table and bent forward to examine the space on the shelf. Megan immediately saw the problem. A metal lever was blocking the area. She leaned forward and unsuccessfully tried to push the lever toward the side. She then tried to turn or twist it away with no success. Frustrated, she pushed it backward with more force than she intended and was surprised when she felt the metal give. She heard a small click and felt a rush of stale air.

"What the hell?" She jumped backward and stared at the bookcase. Nick and Nathan heard the surprise in her voice and rushed over to help.

"What happened?"

"I don't know. I was examining the books and found a lever behind the bookshelf. When I pushed it, something moved." Megan looked up at Nick, excitement creeping into her voice. "Do you think this could be what we're looking for?"

Nick shrugged as he and Nathan stepped closer to examine the bookshelf. They immediately found a gap. Nick wrapped his fingers around the edge of the shelf and pulled it forward. The bookcase was heavy as the shelves were full, but it moved noiselessly toward them as he gently pried it open. Their mouths opened in astonishment as they saw the gap in the wall.

Nathan crossed himself. "Damn, I never thought I would see something like this in person."

CHAPTER 3

"What's back there?" Megan asked as she stepped closer to the wall. They looked into the gap, but couldn't see much. Stale air pumped out of the hole toward them.

"Do you have a flashlight?" Nick asked, turning toward her as he spoke.

"Yes, in my grandmother's office. Let me run and get it." Megan left the room with Dudley hot on her heels.

"On the double," Nick teased as he tried to pierce the darkness with the light from his smartphone. Although a few shapes became illuminated, they couldn't see much.

"We'd better wait until she gets back," Nathan said. "Some rooms built in the past had trap doors or weak floors or weren't built as sturdy as they should have been. I wouldn't go in there without some light."

"No argument here," Nick said as he glanced at the door, waiting for Megan to return.

After a few minutes, she appeared with a heavy-duty flashlight. "This should work." She handed it to Nick who immediately turned it on and pointed the beam toward the gap. Dudley stood behind the group and whimpered as they continued their quest.

The trio investigated the darkness like small children spying on a neighbor's yard for the first time. After a few exclamations of disbelief, they all talked and gestured at once.

"I've lived here my entire childhood and never knew this existed," Megan said as she struggled to see inside.

"Point the light down at the floor," Nathan instructed. "Let's see if there are any holes."

Nick did as he was told and found a hardwood floor which appeared to be an extension of the library floor. Years of darkness and unmonitored temperature left the wood with a different color, but it appeared to be as solid as the floor upon which they stood. Nick placed his foot on the floor and pressed down as hard as possible while he held the doorframe with one hand and the flashlight with the other. "Looks and feels pretty solid. Let me take a step or two inside." He turned to Megan who had pulled out her smartphone and was trying to take a photo, but the room was too dark. "Stay here until I can check the floor and see if there are any windows or lights."

Nick slowly advanced into the dark space. He stopped and swept the flashlight back and forth. After a few minutes, he excitedly called out, "You have to see this room. It looks like a time warp."

Nathan and Megan leaned forward and looked through the space in the wall. Megan put her phone down as Nick turned toward them. "I'll shine the light on the floor. Megan, slowly make your way over to me."

Megan walked carefully toward Nick. The air smelled stale, and she brushed away numerous cobwebs on her way. When Nick pointed the flashlight toward the wall, she spied a closed, old-fashioned rolltop desk. Near the desk was a worktable made of wood, covered with small bottles of oil. A writing pen and a dried bottle of ink sat on the corner of the desk. Yellowed paper sat next to the pen, indicating the desk had been used to write in the past.

"I wonder who all this stuff belonged to," Nick said as he swung the light toward Megan.

"I have no clue," Megan said. "We have to find better lighting and check it out. I would assume my great-grandfather, John, or my grandfather, George. Maybe some of the things have identification, which would help."

"You don't remember ever seeing this room?"

Megan slowly shook her head back and forth. "No, I would have remembered. When my parents were fighting, I would find any nook or cranny where I could hide. This spot would have been perfect. Finding that lever was a fluke."

"Don't disturb anything," Nathan shouted out. "You need to mark the room before you move a thing. The position of the items in the room could be significant." Nathan leaned toward Nick and reached for the flashlight. "May I?"

"Of course, be my guest," Nick said as he handed it over.

Nathan took the flashlight and whistled as he directed the beam in front of him. "A secret room. How great is that? I don't see an exit, but it's hard to tell. Maybe there's a door to a tunnel."

"A secret tunnel from the library?"

"For all we know, this room could have been a storage closet which led to the cellar in some fashion," Nathan said as he looked toward Megan. "Do you know if this house has a cellar?"

"I know there's a stairway in the pantry which leads to a room under the kitchen. I went down there a couple of times when I was a kid, but I thought it was creepy, so I avoided it whenever I could."

"What was down there?" Nick asked.

"I don't know," Megan said. "Supplies and things, I suppose. Maybe beach stuff. The floor was made of dirt and smelled funny. My grandmother used to go down there."

"Did she go downstairs from any other part of the house," Nathan asked excitedly.

Megan shrugged her shoulders although no one could see her in the dark. "I don't know. I wasn't with her twenty-four hours a day." She paused for a second. "Can we get out of here? This room is giving me the creeps."

"Of course," Nathan replied. "We should go back into the library and make some plans. There may be wonderful treasures stored in here."

"Including spiders and bugs and other creepy things," Megan said as she grabbed Nick's hand. He pulled her close and squeezed her hand.

"Don't worry. I'll protect you."

"Great, but do it out there." Megan made her way toward the light on the other side of the hole in the wall.

CHAPTER 4

The trio blinked as they came from the dark room into the library. "That was random and unexpected," Nathan said as he brushed cobwebs off his shoulders.

Dudley ran to Megan and pushed his nose against her leg, happy she was back in the library. She bent forward and scratched him behind the ears. "I'm okay, baby. It's all good, try to relax." Megan stood and brushed the top of her head. After a moment she turned around. "Nick, please look in my hair." She turned her back toward him. "Are there any spiders or creepy things?"

Nick chuckled as he brushed the top of her head. "I don't see anything except for dust bunnies."

Megan shuddered and hugged herself. "I was imagining things crawling on me. It was freaking me out."

"You look fine, so relax," Nick said.

Megan squinted at Nick and turned to Nathan. "Now what do we do?"

"Well, that would be up to you. It's your house. I would recommend we explore the room as quickly as possible. There could be a significant find in there. How much do you know about your great-grandfather?"

"Not much," Megan said as she shrugged. "I know he was a sea captain. I already told you what I know about the history of Misty Manor. Beyond that, I don't know much about my great-grandfather or my grandfather."

"Earlier, you said they had grand parties in the house?"

"Yes, I did," Megan nodded.

"Perhaps this room was used to hide treasures so none of the guests could steal anything when they visited?" Nathan suggested.

"I suppose that's possible."

"Maybe there are important documents or deeds in there," Nick suggested.

"Jimmy Hoffa could be in there for all I know," Megan said with raised eyebrows. "So, what do we do next?"

Nathan thought for a moment. "Let's get some lights, go back in and see what we find." He turned toward Megan. "I know I have no right to be in on this, but I'd love to be here when you do. I think you were right when you started taking photos. You'll need to document our entry to capture any important discoveries. By the way, I wouldn't tell anyone else about the room until it's official and you've secured everything you find. You have no idea what kind of people come out of the woodwork when they hear about treasure."

Megan laughed. "I don't need a reason to bring strange people into this house, Nathan."

"I guess we should close this door," Nick said as he grabbed the edge of the bookcase and pushed it toward the wall.

"Do you think we'll have any problem getting it open again?" Megan asked as she watched.

Nathan shook his head. "It looks like a simple lever mechanism. It's amazing it's been here and kept secret all this time."

"That shows how many people are pulling books off these shelves and reading them," Megan pointed out. "With that in mind, I don't want to put an original 135-year-old version of *Treasure Island* back on the bookshelf if we're going to keep pulling it out. Maybe we can put a phone book there or something else for now."

"It's not my business, but you should hide the lever more securely until you come back. Putting a phone book near original classics will surely draw someone's attention."

"I guess you're right," Megan said as she looked at the books. "Okay, I'll leave *Treasure Island* on the desk and move the classic dictionary into its place." Megan rearranged the shelf. "I'm going to have to speak to someone about the best way to preserve these books. I don't think they should be sitting on the shelves, exposed to sun and air."

"I agree, and I have a name of a book historian you can use. I have a friend at Princeton University who may be able to help."

"That would be great," Megan said. She picked up the volume of *Treasure Island* and gently placed it on the desk. She placed the dictionary on the shelf. It was a perfect fit to hide the lever.

Nathan looked at his watch. "I'd better run. I have another appointment this afternoon." He looked up at Megan and Nick. "Do you have any idea when you might reopen the bookcase? I'd like to be here when you do."

Megan shrugged and looked to Nick for guidance. "Today is Thursday. I guess it depends on Nick's work schedule between now and the weekend. He's going to have to help me set up lights, then camera and action."

Nick frowned as he looked around. "I'm working later tonight and then again tomorrow. The soonest I could get back here is Saturday morning. I have some lighting units we use for emergencies. I could bring one along and set it up."

Nathan raised his eyebrows. "I'm free on Saturday. There's nothing I can't reschedule at this point." He turned to Nick. "I'll help you set up whatever you need."

"Sounds great," Nick said as he nodded.

Nathan smiled wide and clapped his hands together. "I can't wait. This discovery is exciting."

"Then I'd better call Teddy and let him know what's going on," Megan said. "He should probably be here for the big reveal. Who knows what we're going to find?"

"It's a date then," Nick said. "Everyone will meet back here, Saturday morning at ten o'clock sharp."

CHAPTER 5

 egan rinsed her hands with warm water in the kitchen sink and dried them on a nearby towel. She was racking her memory, trying to recall whether her grandmother had ever mentioned anything about a secret room or hidden treasures. Megan had never known her great-grandparents and had no specific memory of conversations about anything to do with the things her great-grandfather may have collected on his voyages. Surely, if she had known there was a secret room, she would have searched every inch of it as a child. Megan wondered if Rose knew there had been another room off the library.

She placed the towel on a counter and wondered how many other secrets Misty Manor held. She was beginning to think there were plenty which she never comprehended as a child.

"Penny for your thoughts?" Megan jumped as Marie entered the kitchen holding a bag of groceries. A stalk of celery was sticking up from the top. In her other hand, she held a tote bag stuffed full of milk and juices. Megan ran over and helped her place her bags on the kitchen table.

"Is there anything else outside?" Megan asked as she looked up at Marie.

"No, I only bought what I needed for tonight's dinner. I would've done those dishes, but I had to run out. You looked like you were lost in thought when I walked in."

Megan smiled. "You know me, Marie. I'm always finding something to worry about."

"Having problems with the architect?"

Megan froze for a moment but then realized Marie was aware she was meeting with Nathan to go over the blueprints. The only people in the house when they found the secret room were herself, Nick and Nathan but now she realized she would have to plan for Saturday morning. She didn't want a house full of people when they finally lit the room or passage or whatever it was they found. Nathan was smart in suggesting they keep the discovery under wraps. The last thing she wanted was another rumor running around town. Although, the folks in the community were kinder and more supportive than the mayor. Still, the rumor mill was active and very creative in Misty Point.

Megan frowned and shook her head. "Let's say today didn't go the way I'd hoped. We have more work to do before we're ready to make plans, apply for permits and start picking out supplies."

Marie laughed. "Working with architects and contractors is probably as close to torture as you can get. Projects start small and grow by leaps and bounds."

"Day one and the plans have already changed."

"That's normal," Marie reassured her. "The project will take on a life of its own. Sit back and enjoy the ride or as my grandmother would say, buckle up, things are going to get bumpy."

A lovely chime began to ring in Megan's back pocket. She pulled out her phone and answered, "Hello?"

"Megan, where are you? I thought you were coming to the beach this morning."

"Georgie?" Megan looked at her watch and realized it was past noon. "I'm sorry. I got pulled into something and let the time get away from me."

"Whatever, but if you want to watch the surf contest, you'd better get here soon."

"Okay, I'm on my way. Try not to do anything fancy until I get there."

"I can't stop the waves. Hurry up. Amber will be waiting for you at our usual gate."

"Alright, let me go." Megan disconnected the call and shoved the phone back in her pocket. She turned to see Marie taking groceries out of her bags and organizing them on the counter. "I'm running down to the beach to watch the surfing contest."

"Sounds like fun." Marie looked down to see Dudley watching her with interest. Each time she took an item out of the bag, the dog's eyes followed her hand until she placed it on the kitchen table. "Are you taking your friend with you?"

"I don't think so," Megan said as she shook her head. "It appears he has a sudden interest in what you're doing with all that food. Besides, there are a lot of spectators including my favorite mayor at the contest, and I don't want anyone complaining about Dudley."

"Okay, I'll keep an eye on him. I'm sure he'll enjoy cooking with me," Marie said as she smiled.

"Don't feed him too much. Boxers will never say no, and I don't want him to get fat."

"Don't worry about the dog," Marie said as she shooed her out the door. "I promise he'll stay healthy. Now go and enjoy the day with your friends."

Not wanting to be late, Megan left the house and ran to the boardwalk.

CHAPTER 6

*A*mber looked up when she saw her friend approach. She pointedly checked her watch. "Nice of you to show up."

Megan stopped running. Bending forward, she spent a few moments sucking fresh air into her lungs.

"You're going to have to run more if you want to get into shape." Amber grinned as she leaned against the boardwalk railing.

"Shut up, will you?" Megan frowned at her friend as she turned toward the water. "Where's Georgie?"

Amber pointed to the left side of the beach. "She's waiting down there for the second heat."

"I see her," Megan said as she spotted her friend holding her freshly waxed surfboard. Wearing her favorite wetsuit, Georgie patiently waited with her group. Megan turned back to Amber who was predictably wearing a designer swimsuit with a matching cover. "Do you plan on going in the water?"

"Are you kidding? It's early in the season. The water temperature is barely out of the fifties."

"I wasn't sure," Megan said as she looked at Amber's swimwear. "That's a gorgeous suit."

Amber pulled the sash around the cover into a tight knot. "Oh, thanks." Leaning toward Megan, she whispered. "There's always a ton of local media at this event. I wanted to make sure I looked okay if I wound up in the background of any of the photos. Plus, I can get started on my tan."

"Are you still doing that with all the talk about skin cancer these days?" Megan asked.

Amber laughed and pulled out her sunscreen. "I've got the right lotion. I don't want a dark tan, but I don't want to look like I saw a ghost."

Megan shielded her eyes from the sun and turned back to Georgie. "I think Georgie said her new wetsuit has a UPF over 50. I ran out of the house so fast, I forgot to wear my sunglasses, so I'll be getting cataracts before either of you."

Amber rolled her eyes and laughed. "I think you're going to want to lose the jeans and sneakers at some point as well. I'm sure you've inherited enough money to buy new clothes. I know last year was crazy with Grandma Rose being sick and all, but it's a new year, and you have to start getting back into the swing of things here in Misty Point."

Megan looked at Amber and smiled. Her friends knew she inherited Misty Manor instead of her father. Had her father inherited the property, he would have sold it to make a quick buck. Thankfully, no one except Teddy and Jonathan knew she had inherited two hundred million dollars in addition to the house, and as Amber pointed out so delicately, they would never guess from her clothing.

"Since I've been away so long, tell me how this surfing competition works again," Megan said.

"Really?"

"Yes. I've been in Detroit for seven years. There's not much surfing going on there."

"Ok," Amber said, shrugging her shoulders. "The surfers all break into groups, and each group surfs for the duration of their heat. Depending on how many groups there are, it may only be twenty or thirty minutes. They stay out there and catch the best waves possible. Every run is scored on a ten-point scale by the judges." Amber pointed to a table in the center of the beach which sat under a tent emblazoned with a popular beer company logo. "They take your best two scores and whoever has the highest score wins the heat. There are more specific rules for scoring in the professional leagues, but you get the picture."

"Yes, I remember now." Megan nodded as she took in the entire beach scene. "I know they've held this competition for many years, but for some reason, I never watched it as a kid."

Amber smiled. "Back then, Doogie Portman won every single year. That guy was fantastic on a board."

"Yes, I do remember him. Whatever happened to him?"

Amber held up three fingers and pointed to the judge's table. "He doesn't surf in competitions anymore, but today he is Judge number three."

Megan looked back toward the judge's table. "Oh, wow. That's wild. I never would have recognized him."

"Well, he's aged a bit. He never left the beach. He surfs, snorkels, and scuba dives. Tommy told me he works with some of the fishing charters, but his whole life is the beach. Sometimes, the library pays to have him give a community lesson for the kids on sea life. He's quite the character."

Megan nodded as she watched him get comfortable in his beach chair. "That's interesting."

The pair looked up when the music escalated. Within minutes, an announcer encouraged the next wave of surfers to set up for their heat. Georgie lifted her board and followed three men into the water. They spread out and paddled into the ocean. Within minutes, they floated on their boards while waiting for the perfect wave.

In the meantime, favorite beach songs played over loudspeakers while fans patiently watched for waves. Vendors were selling iced beverages, grilled hot dogs, pizza and ice cream on the boardwalk. The smell of funnel cake and French fries was intoxicating. Fans who were there for the whole day saved room for the seafood festival which was to start in several hours.

Georgie had several good rides. Megan and Amber cheered her on as she caught wave after wave. The judges sat at the table, occasionally using binoculars, as they watched the competitors. Raw scores were posted on occasion although the final tally would have to wait until the end of the day. The weather was beautiful and the ocean perfect as it sent nice sized waves to pound the shore.

Forty minutes later, the girls waited on the boardwalk while Georgie finished her heat, came out of the water and set her board. She grabbed a towel, dried off and ran up to meet them.

"It looked like you had some nice runs," Megan said.

"The winner as far as I'm concerned," Amber chirped in.

Georgie laughed as she threw the towel on the bench. "I don't know. The competition is getting younger every year."

"Yes, but they have less experience. It takes a while to develop your kind of style." The group turned at the male voice to see Doogie Portman walk up behind them and approach Georgie. "Nice job out there today."

Georgie was silent for a moment. She was immediately starstruck hearing Doogie speak.

"Thanks, I mean, wow, uh."

Megan and Amber laughed as they watched Georgie. "She can speak English and eventually will put together a sensical string of words." Megan reached out and offered her hand to Doogie. "I'm Megan Stanford, this is Amber Montgomery, and as you must know from the program, the tongue-tied lifeguard is Georgie Coles."

"Great to meet you all," Doogie said as he shook their hands.

"It's fantastic to meet you," Georgie finally said. "I've watched you surf for years. You're spectacular on a board."

Doogie smiled. "Maybe years ago. I can still handle waves, but not in the competitions. I'm happy to be a judge."

"Oh, are you allowed to talk with me?" Georgie asked with concern.

"Yes, at this point, the scores are all in, but you'll have to wait for the outcome. I was coming up for a cold drink and thought I'd let you know you've got great style."

"Not surprising," Amber said. "She's lived at the beach for the last thirty years. That's how she knows you."

Georgie turned and shot Amber a laser stare to get her to shut up.

"Is that so?" Doogie asked as he turned back to Georgie. "I'm glad to hear it because I'm spending the summer in Misty Point. I'm looking forward to seeing you out here. Maybe we can catch some waves together."

"That would be great."

"It's a date," Doogie said as he turned and walked to the boardwalk for a drink.

CHAPTER 7

Georgie turned back to her friends. She wasn't sure what to say first. "I can't believe it." Then she turned to Amber. "Are you nuts? The guy is famous."

"Oh, please," Amber said. "He went out of his way to offer a compliment. You don't walk away from that. You're his style, and it won't be long before you're both enjoying a cold glass of wine and boiled shrimp while watching a sunset over the bay."

Georgie blushed. Words would not come.

"Wow, he got to you, didn't he?" Megan squeezed her friend's arm. "Why don't we take it day by day. You had a great heat, Georgie. I've got to say that. Why don't we celebrate tonight? Let's get the group together and do something."

Georgie frowned. "I'd love to go out, but I can't tonight. I'm expecting to crash in about thirty minutes, but I also pledged to help with the pirate treasure hunt for the kids."

"Treasure hunt?" Megan asked intrigued. "What's that all about?"

"It's one of the activities which caps off the town fun day," Georgie explained as she pointed toward the poster attached to the boardwalk pole. "We have a committee which organizes the treasure hunt. The kids get a map and an eye patch along with a fake tattoo, sword and a pirate hat. They must follow the clues, all within a contained area of the beach, to find crossed bones and more clues. If they find gold coins along the way, they can turn them in for chocolate, wrapped in gold foil as long as they don't have an allergy to chocolate."

"That sounds exciting," Megan said as she pointed to the poster. "Is there a buried treasure?"

Georgie laughed. "Yes, eventually they'll find a buried treasure filled with beach toys. There's an actual large X made with black sand." Georgie looked up at the group. "You know, X marks the spot."

"We get it," Amber said with a shrug. "The whole thing sounds very cute. I wonder if I can get my company to be a sponsor next year."

Georgie smiled before she continued. "The Captain drags the chest up to the boardwalk where the kids get to pick prizes while they enjoy a cold root beer since they're a bit young for rum."

"That would be a problem," Megan said nodding her head.

"Yes, it would be. The Captain can't have rum since he fell last year. He lost his depth of vision and tripped, so this year, he doesn't get an eye patch either, but we're letting him wear the stuffed parrot on his shoulder."

"You're kidding me," Megan said. "That's hysterical."

"Perhaps, but you can't make this stuff up. The treasure hunt is a nice activity for the kids. We give a prize for the best pirate costume and then we read pirate stories around a bonfire on the beach. It's one of the most popular activities of the summer."

"I can only imagine," Megan said. "Let us know if you need help next year."

"You two want to be camp counselors?"

"Well," Amber paused. "I'd rather get my company to sponsor the treasure chest, but it's a possibility."

"Sure, as long as the pirate flag is designer material," Georgie teased.

Amber frowned at Georgie as she flipped her hair in the wind.

Megan reached into her pocket when she felt her cell phone ring. "Hello?"

"Megan, it's me, Nick."

"Hey Nick, what's up?"

"Where are you?"

"I'm on the boardwalk with Georgie and Amber. Georgie just finished her heat, so we're catching up."

"Can anyone hear me?"

"No," Megan said as she shook her head in silence.

"Okay, I wanted to let you know I made arrangements to bring emergency lighting to Misty Manor on Saturday. If there aren't any emergencies in town, I can use one of the generators to set up enough lighting for us to see whatever we need in that room."

"That's great to hear," Megan said, purposely sounding noncommittal to those standing around her.

Nick paused for a second. "Okay, I get it, you can't talk right now. I'll call you later so that we can go over the rest of the details. Did you speak to Teddy yet?"

"No, I haven't heard from him at all," Megan said lightly. "I'll give him a call later today to see how he is."

"Okay. Text me when you get back to the house."

"I will, Nick," Megan whispered as she turned away from her friends. When she turned back toward them, she placed her cell in the pocket of her jacket.

"Looks like you're going to have plans for tonight anyway," Georgie teased.

Megan blushed as she cocked her head to the side. "Looks that way. I don't know what time Nick can visit. It depends on his schedule."

Georgie shook her head. "It's amazing how busy a small coastal police force can be."

"I'll second that," Amber said. "The town is growing. The population used to be mainly summer residents, but most of the people I know are living here year-round now."

"It certainly seems that way," Megan agreed. "Anyway, I'd better get back. Marie started making dinner. I didn't realize the surfing contest was such an organized event for the town, but I'll remember next year."

Amber tightened the wrap around her bathing suit. "I've got to find Tommy and see what he's doing. Have a great time tonight, and we'll meet up soon."

Georgie waved. "Bye ladies, thanks for coming."

CHAPTER 8

"*D*id you know there was a secret room?" Megan asked Teddy as she raised the volume on her cell phone. She perched on the edge of a rocking chair on the front porch of Misty Manor.

"This is the first I've heard of it," Teddy said in a huff. "A secret room in the library?"

"Do you think Rose knew?" Megan looked out at the ocean as she thought about her grandmother. The waves rushed to shore, and the wind felt great against her face. She reached down and scratched Dudley's head as she enjoyed the crisp scent of salty air.

Teddy paused for a moment. "I honestly don't think so. Rose trusted me with almost everything there was to know about Misty Manor. We worked well together and were great friends. I can't imagine her keeping a secret like that."

Megan considered that information carefully. Teddy and Rose had been close friends for many years, yet Megan never realized the extent of their relationship as she was growing up. Rose was crafty when she wanted to be, and Megan felt she could keep a secret but the room they found that morning looked as if it hadn't been disturbed for many years. Probably more years than Rose had lived in Misty Manor.

"Does it matter?" Teddy asked.

"What?" Megan asked, snapping out of her thoughts.

"I wanted to know what difference it makes? At this point, we have no choice but to move forward," Teddy said kindly. He then paused and was silent.

"What are you thinking?" Megan asked after several seconds of dead air.

Teddy sighed. "Deep in my heart, I can't believe Rose knew about the room. She was so precise when she put her will together. She was very specific about certain things in the house. I can't imagine she wouldn't tell me about the room if she knew it existed. Were you able to see anything in the room when you were there?"

"Not much. I saw a rolltop desk. There were various pieces of furniture, and I know it had a wood floor, but I'm not sure if it was clutter or valuable mementos. It doesn't matter. Nick plans to bring lighting, so we can go in there and take a good look. No one else knows about this except you, me, Nathan and Nick. We want to keep a lid on it until we know what we're going to find."

"I wish it could stay that way, but I'm sure there are already questions about why Nick needs the lights, and I've heard of this architect, but I don't know him well. Who knows if we can trust him?"

"Well, it's too late now. If it weren't for Nathan, we never would have known about the room. He's more excited than we are."

"That's what worries me," Teddy said.

"We're planning on opening the room Saturday morning. Would you like to be there? Do you think you need to be there for legal reasons?"

"I don't know that I need to be there, but you need to video the entire event. Don't let anyone touch anything and don't let anyone remove anything from the room. Use the light and take a video of whatever you find. We'll review it and then decide what we need to do next, but don't show it to anyone else."

"There may be nothing but junk in there. Nathan said homes like this used to have a secret room where they stored valuables when they entertained or left the house for the season. My great-grandfather

34

traveled the world in the early 1900's. Who knows what could be in there?"

"That's very true. Something which wasn't valuable back then could be worth a lot more now." Teddy was silent for a moment. "Megan, I can't be there Saturday, but now I think we should have Nathan sign a non-disclosure agreement."

"You think he would?"

"If he's excited about getting a look in the room, he would."

"I'll leave it up to you," Megan said as she gazed at the water. "When would we have him sign?"

"He'll have to sign before we open the room on Saturday," Teddy said. "I can't make it to the house, but I'm going to send Jonathan to oversee the process."

Megan's eyes opened wide as she considered the day. Jonathan Brandon Carter, the very available and attractive son of Theodore Harrison Carter, would be in one room with Nick Taylor. Now that would be interesting. If Jonathan were going to take Teddy's place when he retired, the two of them would have to learn to get along. The trouble was that Nick and Jonathan were not exactly best friends. Both were very interested in Megan. Nick had asked Megan to the prom when they were in high school, and now that she returned to Misty Point, he assured her his love had never died.

Jonathan and Megan had a play date when they were young, which Megan didn't remember until Teddy reminded her. All grown up, Jonathan was a handsome, successful attorney who had schooled at Oxford. He was also very single. Many people thought both men were interested in Megan due to her inheritance although only Teddy and Jonathan knew she was now worth over two hundred million dollars. Bringing the two together would be quite interesting.

"Did you set a time for Saturday?" Teddy asked, forcing Megan to snap back to the conversation.

"10:00 a.m. sharp. Nick will probably come earlier to bring the generator or lights or whatever. Nathan will probably show up early as well."

"Fine, I'll tell Jonathan to arrive around 9:00 a.m. I'll talk to him

35

about bringing the agreement and a camera. He'll have to video the event. Otherwise, we'll have another person to worry about signing a non-disclosure agreement and keeping silent."

Megan laughed. "We're going to go through all this trouble and find out nothing more than old furniture is stored in there."

"Maybe or maybe not," Teddy said with a sigh. "There are many things we don't know yet, especially when it comes to Misty Manor."

"What do you mean?" Megan asked as she shifted position.

"That's the point, I don't exactly know," said Teddy as he laughed. "Rose left things for you which we haven't started dealing with yet. There are letters and even a collection of videos. Before you ask, they're sealed, so I have not read or viewed anything. I have no idea what the content is. She did leave instructions about when to give each item to you."

Megan was flustered. "I'm confused, Teddy. If she left things for me, I should be able to access them. What kind of restrictions? There may be important information about Misty Manor."

"The instructions were more about giving you documents or videos after your first Board of Trustees meeting. I imagine Rose thought the information didn't carry much value if you decided not to follow her footsteps."

"But I did choose to take her place, so we need to discuss these items. I should have a list of documents or videos in case something ever happens to you."

"Jonathan will carry out the directive if I disappear but that's a whole different issue. In the meantime, Jonathan will be there Saturday morning, and we'll know for sure what's hidden in that room. I've got to run to a meeting, but I'll talk to you after the weekend. Be careful, Megan. Keep as much of this information as quiet as possible. Even if there is nothing in the room but furniture, the mere fact there is a secret room will cause a stir when left in the minds of the community."

"I understand," Megan said as she waited for Teddy to click off the call. Shifting back into her rocking chair, she considered what he said, and then spent the rest of the day in wary anticipation.

CHAPTER 9

On Saturday morning, Megan paced in the foyer as she waited for everyone to arrive. She was tired. She went to bed the evening before and only slept for a few hours. She woke up, full of anxiety, on the fringe of an intense dream about being lost in the dark. In her dream, someone was chasing her, but she didn't know who or why. She jumped up, her heart racing, and was unable to fall back to sleep. She tossed and turned, reviewed the hundreds of thoughts which danced through her head and made resolutions which she promptly forgot when the sun rose.

She dressed for the day in typical jeans and a t-shirt, expecting the secret room to be dirty or dusty. With hours to spare, she took Dudley outside for a run along the beach after he made a pit stop near the weeds. Smiling, she watched as he pranced back and forth, chasing seagulls as they played along.

Megan was glad she owned a private beach on the cape of Misty Point. It allowed her the freedom of walking, running her dog and relaxing with a cup of coffee as she enjoyed the calming sound of crashing waves as well as the healing scent of the sea.

When they arrived back at the house, Megan fed the pets and waited for another strong pot of coffee to brew. She made a full pot expecting others would want a cup when they arrived. Pouring a nice sized mug, she added cream, sugar, and cinnamon. Marie would have made the first pot of coffee for the day, but Megan asked her to take the day off from cleaning and cooking to keep the spectators to a minimum. Even so, things still felt like they were spiraling higher than necessary.

Holding her coffee with two hands, she paced the foyer in anticipation of a disastrous day. Within minutes, the doorbell rang. Megan opened the front door to find Jonathan Brandon Carter standing in front of her. He was wearing an designer suit, expensive cologne and carried a large wide briefcase.

"Hi, Jonathan," Megan said as she pulled back the door and gave Dudley a command. He sat at attention and didn't approach their visitor.

Jonathan's face lit up with a 1000-watt smile as he crossed the threshold. He leaned forward and kissed her on the cheek. "Megan, it's great to see you."

Megan blushed as she nodded. She was genuinely pleased to see him. She had heard the rumors of his friendship or attraction being a result of her inheritance, but Megan felt his warmth was honestly generated by more than the bottom line in her checking account.

He was wearing a modest Ralph Lauren suit. "You look great, Jonathan. London must be treating you well."

"Yes, it was nice to go back. I can't believe it's been three months, but most of my business is wrapped up now and has been handed over to my partners. I'd be fibbing to say I wouldn't miss England. I still have my flat there. There are a few more things to do, and I plan to visit regularly, but I need to help my father, so I'll be spending a lot more time in America. Have you ever been, Megan?"

Megan gave her head a slight shake. "I'm sorry?"

"To London? Have you ever been abroad?"

Megan smiled. "The farthest I've been from home is Detroit."

Jonathan lifted his eyebrows in surprise. "You'll have to do something about that very soon. Perhaps you'll come with me for the next trip over the pond?"

Megan blushed as she laughed. "We'll see. I have quite a bit to accomplish here this summer. I've just come back to the Jersey Shore. It may be a bit premature to leave again."

Jonathan squeezed her shoulder. "Think about it. You can certainly leave for a week or two come late fall."

"I promise to think about it," she said as she nodded her head although she couldn't visualize traveling through London with Jonathan for two weeks. Nick certainly wouldn't be happy. She pointed to his suit and said, "I hope this little adventure doesn't mess your suit. I have no idea what's in this room or how dirty it will be."

"Fortunately, I'm only handling documents and the camera. Although, I'm ready to pitch in if they need some muscle." Jonathan flexed his arm and Megan couldn't help laughing at the bravado. He was by no means a small man but was always so formal she couldn't imagine him doing physical labor such as moving a couch or boxes. She chided herself for judging him. Perhaps she had simply never seen him in those situations.

"I'm sorry, I didn't mean to laugh, but I can't see you performing heavy labor in that suit." Megan turned toward the library and beckoned him to follow her. "Why don't you bring your things into the library, so you'll be ready when Nathan gets here. Would you like a cup of coffee?"

"I'm fine for the moment, but I might have some tea a bit later if that's alright." He followed her into the library, and as he was placing his briefcase on the table, they heard the doorbell ring. They both turned to look at the foyer at the same time.

"Marie isn't here today so let me go answer that while you get your papers ready."

Jonathan nodded and turned to his briefcase as Megan left the room. Dudley followed her and once again obeyed her command. She reached the front door and opened it to find Nathan standing on the threshold. He was wearing jeans and an open collar button down shirt. He was smiling with his hands shoved in his front pockets, rocking back and forth on his feet. "Nathan, how are you? Please, come in."

"Thanks, I hope I didn't come too early."

"No, this is fine. There's someone in the library who wants to speak with you before we start this whole process."

Nathan looked confused as she drew him into the library and introduced him. "Please meet Jonathan Brandon Carter. He's Teddy's son and is representing him today. Unfortunately, Teddy couldn't be here."

Nathan leaned forward and shook hands with Jonathan. "It's very nice to meet you, but I'm afraid I don't understand."

"Please have a seat," Megan said as she pulled out a chair and looked at the two men. "I believe you told me to let Teddy know what was going on and I did. He says he didn't know anything about a room off the library and Rose never mentioned one to him. But, in case something important showed up, he thought it should be on video and asked Jonathan to have you sign a paper."

"What kind of paper?"

"It's a non-disclosure agreement," Jonathan joined in. "It states that regardless of what we find or don't find, you agree not to reveal any information to anyone, in any format, including the existence of a secret room."

Nathan raised his eyebrows. "That covers it all, I think."

"It's a general agreement," Jonathan said. "It also states that you have no claim or rights to anything that may be found in the room or as a result of opening the room."

Nathan laughed as he shook his head. "You have to calm down, Buddy. I'm an architect, and I specialize in Grand Victorian houses. I want to see the room for historical purposes. I didn't think I was walking out of there with anything."

Jonathan smiled and bent his head forward, ever so subtly. "If Miss Stanford decides to publicize the room or show it on tour, she may decide whether to release your agreement at that time for commentary."

Megan's head snapped around to Jonathan. "Tour? What do you mean tour?"

Jonathan shrugged. "You never know, Megan. Once Misty Manor

is returned to its full splendor, you may have magazines who'll want to do a feature on the house. There are grand estates which make a lot of money from tours through their home, especially near Christmas when the decorations are up. Perhaps Misty Manor will become a bed and breakfast one day. There are many possibilities."

As surprised as Nathan felt, Megan blinked a couple of times. "Thanks, but no thanks. I want to live in the house with Dudley and Smokey. I'm not looking for anything but rest now. That and some stress-free beach days so I can relax and get on with life."

"Noted, but we're covering ourselves for the future." Jonathan turned toward Nathan and handed him the agreement and a pen. "Please take some time to read it through before you sign."

Rubbing her forehead, Megan stood up from the table. "If you'll excuse me, I'd like to get the coffee ready in case anyone needs a cup." She turned and left the room with Dudley on her heels.

CHAPTER 10

Ten minutes later, Megan returned to the library with a large tray and Dudley in tow. On the tray, she had several coffee mugs as well as a beautiful china teacup with a matching saucer. Jonathan rushed over to help her. He took the tray from her and placed it on the table. Megan quickly unloaded placemats, cream, sugar, mugs and teacup, a full carafe of strong, rich coffee, and a ceramic pot of hot water with several different containers of loose tea. She also added a small plate of biscotti.

"Looks delicious," Jonathan said, clearly impressed.

"Thank you. I only have four flavors of tea," Megan said as she arranged them. "Mint Green, Peach Apricot White Tea, Mango Oolong and Earl Grey. I hope one of them meets your fancy."

Jonathan laughed as he chose the Earl Grey. "It's still a bit early in the morning. Earl Grey will be fine. Have you ever had high tea?"

"Excuse me?"

"I was wondering if you'd ever had high tea somewhere?" Jonathan smiled. "It's quite relaxing. Delicious tea with small little sandwiches in the afternoon."

Megan smiled. "No, I can't say I've ever done that."

"Some wonderful hotels in New York City put on a fancy tea. Perhaps we can go one day?

"Sounds like it would be fun."

"I promise it would be," Jonathan said.

Blushing, Megan turned to Nathan. "Would you like coffee or tea?"

Nathan frowned as he slid the paper and pen over toward Jonathan's briefcase and stood. "Coffee please, with cream and sugar. It smells delicious. If it weren't so early, I'd be adding something else to enhance the flavor."

Megan looked at him and grinned. "I have a few things in the liquor cabinet if you'd like to choose something." The tension broke, Nathan smiled and took the mug Megan offered him. "I'm fine for now. Very much appreciated, thank you."

The trio enjoyed their drinks and eventually heard a knock at the front door. Megan and Dudley went to answer and found Nick on the threshold. He crossed into the room, holding a rectangular metal box which was a little larger than a phone book. Dudley was excited and jumped until Nick rubbed his head. At the same time, Nick leaned forward and gave Megan a quick kiss. "I saw cars out there. I assume someone's here?"

Megan rolled her eyes and whispered. "Oh yes, they're in the library having coffee and tea. I told Teddy what we were doing, and he insisted Jonathan come to video the event. He also insisted that Jonathan have Nathan sign a non-disclosure agreement about what we find and even the presence of the room."

"Get the hell out," Nick said with a snort. He leaned toward her and whispered, "He'd better not ask me to sign anything because it's not happening."

Megan rolled her eyes. "Having all of you together is stressing me out."

"We should have done this by ourselves," Nick said as he shook his head.

"Hey, you were the one who announced you couldn't come back until Saturday morning and you said it right in front of Nathan." Megan huffed with her hands on her hips.

"I know, I know." Nick pressed his forehead against Megan's as he hugged her. "I'm sorry. I promise I'll make it up to you somehow."

"Hmmn," Megan said as she frowned. "I'm going to hold you to that."

"Good, I'm looking forward to it," Nick grinned as Megan blushed.

She pointed to the library. "Let's go."

Nick walked into the library followed by Megan and Dudley. He walked toward the cherrywood table and placed the item he was holding on the floor. "Gentlemen, how are you today?"

Jonathan stood and held out his hand. "Doing fine, Nick, how are you?" He was courteous but not overly friendly.

Nick shook his hand. "Little busy these days, but I'm well. How about you? I haven't seen you around in a while."

"Yes, I was away on business."

Nick turned to Nathan and shook his hand as well. "Excited?"

"I have to admit the curiosity is overwhelming," Nathan said as he nodded his head.

"Well let's get to it then." Nick bent down and picked up his metal box as Megan followed close behind. She sent Dudley to his blanket on the side of the room where he patiently watched the activity.

"What is that?" Megan asked as he watched Nick set the box down near the bookshelf.

"Emergency lighting. The police department uses it to light up active scenes at night. We can plug it in or use the battery pack if we want."

"Will it be strong enough?" Megan asked.

"You'll be surprised how bright this is. Don't look at it once we light it up."

"I don't think you have to worry about that," Nathan said. "We'll be looking elsewhere."

Nick approached the bookshelf and then turned back to find Megan. "Are we ready to start?"

"I guess so," Megan said as she looked at Jonathan. "Are you ready?"

He raised his phone and gave a thumbs up. "The camera on this phone is better than a hand-held camera, so we're good. But, if necessary, I've got a portable action camera in my briefcase."

"Okay, then let's do this," Megan said as she looked at Nick.

"It's your library," Nick said as he smiled at Megan. "You have the honor of opening the bookcase."

Once Jonathan started filming, Megan approached the bookcase and pulled out the large dictionary. Jonathan narrated the date, time and actions as he recorded. Placing the dictionary on the nearby table, Megan turned back to the bookcase and pushed on the lever. After hearing a click, she was able to pull the bookcase toward her and reveal the entryway into the secret room.

"Okay, let's stop for a moment," Nick said. He plugged the portable halogen light into a nearby outlet and positioned it toward the doorway. Jonathan ran up to the entrance and held the phone high enough to be able to record the basic layout of the room before it was touched.

The secret room was part of the original library. A faux wall had been made and then concealed by bookshelves. Inside, the floor and walls remained unfinished, but the room contained some furniture and decoration.

A rolltop desk stood off to the left loaded with various compartments and drawers, and Megan couldn't wait to look through them. In front of the desk was an old-fashioned wooden rolling chair. Next to the desk, she saw a table with various bottles of oil, a fountain pen and a dried bottle of ink. There were various paintings on the walls. Megan had no idea if they were simply decorations or valuable treasure. She also spied an old typewriter, small candles, and books piled on the table.

"Can we go in?" Megan asked as she turned to Nick and Jonathan.

"After you," Nick said as he pointed toward the room.

Megan crossed the threshold and ran her fingertips over the edge of the table which was covered by dust. She felt she had stepped back in time. "Except for what we did the other day, this room doesn't look like it's been opened in a long time."

Nick, Jonathan, and Nathan followed her inside. They all slowly turned and examined the items they saw before them. Jonathan shot the group an icy stare. "Please don't touch anything until I've had a chance to video the contents."

Nick turned and rolled his eyes at Megan. His frown said everything about Jonathan's presence. Nick continued to scan the room while Jonathan recorded.

"Here's a kerosene lamp," Nick said as he pointed to the corner. "Now we know how the room was lit." He turned to Jonathan. "Are you getting all this? I wouldn't want you to miss anything."

"Smart man," Jonathan said with a nod. "Thank you."

Nick sidled up to Megan. "This guy wouldn't know sarcasm if it hit him in the face."

Megan reached out and squeezed his fingers before she whispered. "Nick, please behave for now."

Nathan walked over to the wall and examined a calendar from the year 1925. He pointed out the date to everyone. "It's hard to believe they were using all these items almost one hundred years ago. We tend to think people were in the stone age back then but sometimes I think they had a better quality of life than we do now."

Jonathan continued to spin in the middle of the room to catch a 360-degree view which they later could use. Megan walked over to the desk and looked at a photo of a man and a woman standing next to each other. The sepia photo, as well as the clothes worn by the couple, lent the impression the photo was taken in the early 1900's. A handsome man was wearing a dark, heavy woolen suit complete with a double-breasted vest over a high paper collar white shirt. The vest boasted what appeared to be an expensive pocket watch and on his head was a formal Bowler hat. Next to him stood a beautiful woman wearing a satin silk evening gown with a skirt and train trimmed with silk tulle. She wore a corset, and one could see a three-tiered silk bustle in the back. Lace gloves covered her hands, and she held a parasol over her head. The couple appeared to be standing on the porch of Misty Manor, and the ocean was glorious in the background. Megan wished the photo was in color. She could only imagine the satin silk evening gown in a soft shade of pink.

"Nice couple, who are they?" Nick's voice penetrated Megan's thoughts.

"I'm not sure, but I would guess they're my great-grandfather, John Stanford and his wife, Mary Stanford, my great-grandmother."

"They look like they were part of a prominent crowd."

"From everything I hear, they were. My great-grandfather collected treasures worth a lot of money."

"What did he do?" Nathan asked as he walked up to the couple.

"As I mentioned the other day, he was a sea captain," Megan said. "He was sponsored by some very rich people to sail away and bring treasures back to America." She paused as she surveyed the room. "It appears he was rewarded handsomely."

"You can say that again," Nathan said as he nodded his head and looked around the room.

Megan frowned as she watched him. "Well, lucky for us that's not the reason we're in here. We're researching the room as an architectural anomaly, not for its contents."

"Exactly," Nick said. "We're not here looking for treasures."

"That's the reason I'm filming this whole adventure. If there are any treasures, I don't want them to disappear," Jonathan said with a pointed glance at the trio.

"Agreed," Megan said as she continued to look at the desk. There was a journal which had a photo stuck in the front cover. It showed the same man standing on the deck of a ship. He was wearing a uniform of sorts. His hand was casually resting on the captain's wheel, and his feet were crossed at the ankle. He had a broad smile and boasted whiskers on his face. In the background, seagulls flew in the sky over an ocean highlighted by mountains in the distance. "He must have been in a port of some kind."

"Maybe he was happy to find land after a difficult voyage," Nick teased. "Or perhaps he was planning to go ashore for a shave and a haircut."

"I wonder how long a journey across the ocean lasted in the early 1900's," Nathan said.

"I have no clue." Megan reached out and gently opened the cover of the log. The pages were thin and yellowed but contained faded ink written in a bold, fancy style. She leaned forward to take a better look. "Very faint but this log reads…*1912, August 14, set sail for South America. The water looks rougher than usual and will have to….*" She paused, then closed the book and stood up. "I can't read much more without getting a better light and using gloves to make sure we preserve the page."

To the right of the desk, they found a ship bell. It was the size of a basketball. Nick leaned forward to pick it up. "This is a lot heavier than I expected." He gave it a shake which resulted in a very loud peal throughout the room. Nick then rested the bell back on the table.

As they continued to explore, they found a chess set in the corner. An oriental rug covered part of the floor as well as some larger carvings and statues on the side.

"I'll bet those are from his voyages," Nick said.

"I'm sure," Megan agreed. "They all look very exotic. I'll have to check what they're carved from."

"Do you think there's anything under the rug?" Nathan asked as he followed them.

Megan shrugged but didn't lean forward to move the rug. "I'm sure we'll find out eventually."

As they continued down the length of the room, they saw a waist height counter under which hung a velvet curtain. "This looks rather odd. I'll bet there's a fancy garbage pail in there."

"Only one way to find out," Nick said as he turned toward Jonathan. "You getting this?" He slowly pulled the curtain to the side while Jonathan stood directly behind him to capture the moment on video. Nick let out a small whistle. "Hello, what do we have here?"

In front of them stood an old-fashioned Mosler safe complete with a tumbler and lever.

"Holy Moly," Nathan said from behind Megan's shoulder. "Let's open it up." Megan turned to look at him and was suddenly uncomfortable with him being in the room. What had been an architectural find was becoming all too quickly a historical treasure hunt. The safe could contain anything from exotic riches to family photos, but

Nathan's interest now seemed a bit too keen, and he shouldn't have knowledge of all the items in the room.

"I don't think we can," Megan said, hiding her feelings of discomfort. "We'd have to find the combination."

"Let's look through the desk," Nathan said as he pointed to the other side of the room. "Maybe, the combination is in the journal or one of the cubby holes."

Megan began to fan her face. "It's a bit stuffy in here, and I'm getting a little dizzy." She turned to Nick and rolled her eyes, hoping he would catch her meaning. "I think that's enough for one day. This search is a bit overwhelming for me." She turned to Jonathan. "Perhaps we should ask Teddy if he has more information about my great-grandfather before we go digging through all this stuff. Do you know if his estate has any historical papers on file?"

Jonathan shrugged. "I'd have to ask my father. I'm not sure what documentation he has."

"Maybe it would be better to open the safe while everything is being recorded," Jonathan suggested. "We might be able to hear the tumblers click if we listen closely."

Nick looked at Megan and shrugged. Megan checked her watch. "I'll give you five minutes to see if you can open it. Otherwise, I think we're done here for the day."

A whine from the doorway caused the group to look up and see an anxious dog peering in the room. Megan laughed when she saw her dog. "See, Dudley agrees. It's time to call it quits for today."

"Okay, let me give it a quick try," Nick said as he wiggled his fingers. "We had a lecture on lock picking." He quickly dropped down on one knee and leaned forward to place his ear to the safe. Jonathan moved in behind him to allow the camera to get a better view. Nick then rubbed his thumb and first two fingers together and began to turn the dial. Nathan leaned over his other shoulder, so he wouldn't miss any action. Megan crossed her arms over her chest and watched from the side.

After a few turns, Nick pulled back. "I believe we are in business." He reached out, grabbed the lever and twisted it down.

Megan was amazed. "I can't believe you were able to break that combination."

Nick grinned. "To be completely honest, I don't think it was engaged. I love it when they do that in the movies. Some older safes can be easily broken into, and if that fails, you can drill the lock. At any rate, this safe was slightly open, so let's get to it."

Nick pulled the door open when Jonathan leaned forward to get a better view of the contents. He lost his balance and almost landed on Nick's back.

"Hey, get off of me," Nick yelled as Jonathan braced himself with one arm on Nick's back.

"Sorry about that," Jonathan said as he pushed off Nick's back a bit harder than he needed to stand up straight again. Megan watched in shock with raised eyebrows as Nick turned around with a scowl on his face. Nathan stepped back. Megan was sure Nick would have made a gesture or said something vulgar if she weren't in the room.

"Ok, gentleman. Can we get to it?" Megan glared at the three men. "You're like three little kids. I'm going to throw all of you out in a minute."

Nick's jaw clenched as he looked at Jonathan. He then exhaled and turned back to the safe. Reaching out, he pulled the door open then moved out of the way, so Jonathan would have a better view with the camera.

The safe had a few shelves which held various items. A packet of papers tied with string, small carvings, a felt pouch, and jewelry sat on the bottom shelf. However, all eyes were drawn to a small treasure chest, approximately eight inches wide on the top shelf. It was made of wood and had a latch with small leather bindings to keep it secured on the sides and bottom.

"Is that a treasure chest?" Nathan cried out excitedly.

"It sure looks like one," Nick said. "But a miniature version."

"Bring it out, let's open it," Nathan said.

Nick turned to look at Megan who was unhappy at how the entire search was going. Nick pulled out the small treasure chest and placed it on the table. Everyone jockeyed for position, so they could get a better view of the chest. Nick stepped back and allowed Megan to stand right in front of the chest. "You open it. Whatever is in there, belongs to you now."

"Thank you, Nick," Megan said as she stepped forward. She gently opened the latch and lifted the lid. The chest was lined with a soft silk. Resting on a small pillow on the bottom of the chest was a beautiful jade carving of a turtle. Its legs were made of sterling silver.

"How beautiful," she said as she gently touched the jade carving. "I believe this color Jade is somewhat rare." As she picked up the turtle, she was surprised as she held it. "It's heavier than I expected."

"We'll have to get that appraised immediately," Jonathan said as he struggled to get the carving filmed from all sides.

Megan handed the carving to Nick as Nathan shouted out. "Hey, there's something else in the chest."

Megan turned and looked inside. A folded piece of parchment had been resting beneath the turtle. Realizing its age, she gently picked it up and slowly unfolded it for fear it would fall apart.

Fully opened, the yellowed paper revealed lines and squiggles. There were other shapes and marks, but at the bottom right-hand corner was a large X.

"It's a treasure map. I can't believe it, a real treasure map," Nathan shouted out.

Megan looked up at him and then quickly back to the paper. She immediately folded the paper and placed it back into the chest. She then reached for the carving and placed it back in the chest as well. "Okay, I think we're done here for today."

"Are you kidding?" Nathan was shocked when she closed the lid.

"I am not kidding. This search has gotten quite out of control. We had no idea what we were going to find in here, and I think we'd better stop before everything gets further out of control. We need to stop and make a plan of how we're going to handle this." She bent to place the chest back into the safe and then closed the door without locking it.

"You sure we can't look around a bit longer?" Nathan's voice was almost desperate in his attempt to have them continue the search.

"If the lady says we're done, then we're done," Nick said as he folded his arms and shot Nathan a withering look.

Dudley stood at the doorway and began to bark as he sensed the tension in the room.

"Dudley is unhappy," Megan said as she looked toward the dog. "Besides, I think I need some fresh air. We're done for today." She walked toward the doorway as Nathan reluctantly followed.

Nick stood back to allow Jonathan to step in front of him. Jonathan paused. "I want to video the close of the room, so you go first."

Nick laughed and said, "How about this?" He walked toward the doorway and turned to watch Jonathan do another spin of the room with the smartphone. Jonathan began to back out of the room. When he crossed the threshold, Nick snapped off the light and pushed the bookcase back against the wall. Megan walked over and placed the heavy dictionary on the shelf and ushered everyone out of the library for the day.

CHAPTER 11

*M*egan squatted next to the Boxer and scratched his head. "Yes, you're such a good boy protecting me." She stood while the men collected their things and began to walk with them toward the foyer.

"So, what's the next step?" Nathan asked as he turned to look at the group. "Should we schedule another day?"

Jonathan and Nick deferred to Megan.

"I want to talk to Teddy before we do anything else. I don't want to take the room or its contents too lightly. Maybe he'll have some papers or old diaries which would clue us in as to what my great-grandfather used the room for and what's stored in there. Then we'll schedule a date to go back in."

"Sounds reasonable," Nick said as he nodded.

"I'll speak to my father and have him call you," Jonathan said with a smile.

"Make sure you include me," Nathan said excitedly. "I'm more intrigued than ever."

Megan smiled at the men. "As soon as I hear anything, I'll let you all know." She opened the front door and escorted them to the porch.

"Thanks for helping me with my discovery. It's always an exciting day at Misty Manor."

"My pleasure," Nathan said as he reluctantly turned and left the porch.

Neither Jonathan or Nick made a move to leave as each tried to wait the other out. Megan finally turned and said, "Okay guys, I'm going back in. I'll talk to you later."

As she turned, Jonathan quickly stepped up. "I'll call you later and let you know what my father finds."

"Thanks, Jonathan. I'd appreciate that," Megan said. As she looked up at him, he leaned down and kissed her cheek. Nick scowled as he watched.

Nick walked over and kissed her other cheek and whispered. "I'll talk to you soon."

"Thanks, guys. Have a great day." Megan turned, went inside the house and closed the door. Sighing, she leaned against it as Dudley pushed his head against her leg. She knelt and cuddled his head. "Isn't it amazing? I feel like I have three little boys to take care of instead of grown men."

Megan stood up and went to the kitchen to pour herself another cup of dark, rich, coffee. After stirring in cream and sweetener, she called Dudley and headed for the front porch. She wanted to sit in a rocking chair, watch the ocean pound the shore, and smell the salty sea breeze. She was upset with how big of a production opening the room in the library had become. The items in that room, whatever they may be, belonged to her relatives and deserved to be treated as family heirlooms. Megan needed to figure out what she wanted to do with them.

Enjoying her coffee, she ran her fingers through Dudley's fur and watched the seagulls playing over the shoreline. The day was exquisite for May. Blue skies, perfect temperature, and gentle warm breezes. The water was clear and looked almost tropical in the sunlight. Years ago, the waters were darker and muddied with trash, but changes in disposal laws resulted in the water off the coast of New Jersey becoming cleaner and a major tourist site again.

"Hey, got any more of that coffee?"

Megan jumped when she heard the male voice. "Nick, you scared me." She looked down at Dudley. "Neither one of us heard you coming."

"Sorry, I wanted to make sure everyone was gone and then figured I'd circle back to check on you." Nick walked up the front steps of the Grand Victorian. He reached down to pet Dudley who eagerly ran up to meet him. "Why don't you put your coffee down, so we can go for a walk?"

"Sounds like a great idea." Megan placed the cup on the small wicker table next to the rocking chair and stood up. Hand in hand they walked off the porch, over the grass, and down to the sandy beach. Dudley followed them and ran back and forth to the water before chasing seagulls who landed on the sand.

Stopping near the shoreline, they cast off their shoes and walked to the water's edge. The ocean breeze blew Megan's hair as she dipped her feet into the water. Initially, it was a bit chilly but within minutes warmed up to a perfect temperature for them to walk along the water line as the surf crashed back and forth around them.

"So, what are your thoughts about this morning?" Nick asked as he looked at her.

A seagull flew above them, crying out in hopes of a scrap of food. "Nick, it was a circus. I'm sorry we ever found the room, and I'm sorry Nathan has attached himself to our hip. My great-grandfather's possessions are in that room. Whatever they are, they belonged to a man who is a part of me. They may give me a hint of his thoughts, dreams, or hopes when he and my great-grandmother were young. Maybe his journal will speak to the construction of Misty Manor."

"All very true," Nick said as he nodded in agreement.

"I was excited because I wanted to get a glimpse of the people who lived in this house a hundred years before me, but it turned into some weird sort of treasure hunt with no respect to the family."

Facing her, Nick took her hand as the waves swirled around their feet. "I'm happy to hear you say that. Why do you need those two guys hanging around? Is Nathan a friend to Teddy or what's the deal? And don't even get me started about Jonathan." Nick scowled as he mentioned his name.

Megan laughed as she watched his face. "You two aren't going to be close friends?"

Nick frowned again. "The only person I want to be close with is you. I'll do whatever you want to help you with this room or Misty Manor, and I'll admit it's interesting to poke around the house. But don't forget, I was there before you even inherited the house. I'm not there to find treasure. Do we need to keep these guys in the loop? It's your house. Let's do whatever you want, together."

"Thank you, Nick. That's very sweet of you. It's amazing we found a treasure map," Megan said as she smiled. "We have no idea what the treasure is, whether it's pirate booty or some of my great-grandfather's treasures from his voyages, but it may be fun to see what we can find."

Nick's face broke out in a wicked grin. "Pirate booty?"

"Nick...," Megan drew out his name as she turned to face him.

"Sorry, I was thinking about booty."

Megan looked up at Nick and smiled as the surf washed over their legs. The water felt warm and inviting. Nick held her about the waist to steady them and leaned down to kiss her. His lips brushed hers, lightly at first, then with more force and longing. Megan felt her belly tighten as she wrapped her arms around his neck. He massaged her back as he kissed her and then finally pulled back and exhaled against her cheek. "You are beautiful." Megan hugged him tightly and blushed when she realized how his strong embrace thrilled her.

They leaned in for another kiss when they were interrupted by a splatter of water as Dudley dashed into the surf and shook his body. With a canine smile, he looked toward them and barked until they acknowledged him. Laughing, they splashed water toward Dudley who ran far enough away to avoid getting his head wet.

Later, they walked along the surf toward the Point. "Treasures aside, finding this room is exciting because it allows me a small window to see what life was like for my great-grandparents. One hundred years ago sounds like a long time but it's not, and it's amazing how many things have changed in those years. It's amazing what changes have taken place in the last two years, never mind a hundred, but I don't believe they're all positive ones."

"I'm still thinking of booty," Nick said as he watched the seagulls soar around them. They continued to walk, hand in hand down the beach. Dudley continued to splash beside them and run after birds while chasing the waves as they rushed away from the shore.

Megan looked up as they neared the lighthouse. Billy Conklin had been a close friend of her grandparents. He spent his life maintaining the lighthouse and watching over Misty Manor as well as Grandma Rose when Grandpa George went missing. Megan knew he was nearing his mid-eighties and worried about him living in the lighthouse by himself, but when she asked and even offered to find other living arrangements for him, he refused. He'd spent his whole life there and preferred to live out his days by the sea. Megan felt better knowing Amber's boyfriend, Tommy, was Billy's nephew. She was comforted knowing someone else was watching over him, but even so, she wanted to ask if Billy would accept a housekeeper to help him. Megan was willing to pay for the help. Billy watched out for her family, and now it was time to watch out for him, but she had to be careful how she worded her proposal, so Billy wasn't insulted.

As they watched the lighthouse, the front door opened, and Billy, using his favorite cane, ventured out into the sunshine. His shirt and pants looked baggier than the last time Megan saw him. His dark, gray hair was a bit wild.

Megan tugged on Nick's hand. "Hey, let's go see how Billy's feeling. I haven't seen him outside in a long time. I was beginning to worry he couldn't get down the stairs."

"I'll follow you," Nick said. "I'd rather do an informal welfare visit than an official one anytime."

Megan frowned at Nick. "Please, don't say that. I'm constantly worried about him."

Nick held his hands out. "I'm sorry. What do I know? He doesn't look any worse for the wear, but let's check it out." As they walked toward the lighthouse, they watched as Billy stretched and looked out over the beach. He then turned, checked the mailbox near the base of the lighthouse and collected all his mail. From the looks of the pile, he hadn't been outside in several days.

"I wonder if I can get the postal service to do something to make it easier for him to get his mail?"

"You can ask and see what suggestions they make," Nick said. "I know they accommodate a lot of disabilities, but I'm not sure what they do with lighthouses. Someone can always take it out of the box and bring it upstairs for him."

"That's a great idea. I'd better tell Tommy as well, so he can check whenever he comes to visit," Megan said as she watched the elderly gentleman struggle to hold the mail as well as his cane.

When Megan and Nick were close enough, they waved. "Hey Billy, can we help you with that?"

Billy looked up when he heard their voices, surprise evident in his face. A lopsided grin spread across his stubbled face as he waited for them to reach him. "Just in the nick of time," he wheezed as he handed the mail to Nick. "See what I did there? In the nick of time. Get it?"

Nick nodded. "I get it. That's a good one." Nick wrapped his muscled arm around Billy's thin shoulders. "What have you been up to? Getting into trouble out here?"

Billy looked at the young man and frowned. "Wouldn't you like to know? You'd go back to that police station of yours and bring the whole department back."

Nick pursed his lips and nodded. "Billy, with a reputation like yours, I'd have to call for backup. You understand, don't you?"

Billy cackled. "Ain't seen anyone around here for days except all the townies moving back for the summer. I think I'm safe enough, for now, boy."

Nick chuckled as Megan nudged him to the side. "Billy, can we sit on the bench for a few minutes?"

"Guess so, as long as you're gonna help me back up."

"Of course, we will," Megan said as she guided him to a cement bench set in the sand in front of the freshly painted red and white lighthouse. She waited until he picked a part of the bench, turned around and settled himself. Then she and Nick sat down and sandwiched him on either side.

Billy rubbed at his chin with the back of his hand, looked side to side at his visitors and said, "Isn't this mighty cozy? You two happen to be passing by or am I getting set up for something here?"

"We want to talk for a few minutes," Megan said as she squeezed his hand.

"Bout what?" Billy asked suspiciously.

Megan smiled as she watched Billy squint at her. "Honestly, I wanted to make sure you're okay."

"I'm fine," Billy said with a firm nod. "You sure there ain't no but to this?"

"Excuse me?"

"I'm waiting on the but. You know, I'm checking in on you, but as long as I'm here..."

Megan laughed. "Well as long as you're asking, I do have a question." Megan paused as she considered how to proceed.

Billy raised his eyebrows and waited for Megan to collect her thoughts.

"I wanted to ask you about Misty Manor. I'm thinking of doing a little work to modernize things. You probably know the house better than anyone, and I was wondering if there was anything special I should know about the house. Is there anything my grandfather told you about Misty Manor I should know before I get the contractor out here?"

Billy thought for a moment and shook his head. "Nah, not that I can think of." He looked directly at Megan. "I'm really glad to hear you're thinking of keeping the house and fixing things up. Misty's been around a long time, and it'd be a damn shame to see it come down. That house has a lot of history."

"That's why I'm asking you if there's anything special I should know before I start? You're the only person who knows the house better than me at this point. I don't want any surprises."

Billy stared out at the ocean. His eyes appeared to mist. "There's been a lot of history here. Not the same now that your grandmother is gone. Guess I'll be next, but I plan on staying here until the good Lord decides to take me. Why are you asking me a question like that? You got something specific on your mind?"

"No, I want to make sure there's no secret rooms or anything I should know about," Megan said as she shrugged at Nick over Billy's bent head. "I don't want to change anything that makes Misty special plus I'm trying to find out more about my family's history. Did you know my great-grandfather very well?"

"John? Yeah, a great man, he was. Very kind, loving guy. He and Mary were getting on in years when I met your grandfather, but George used to tell me about them. When your grandfather was small, he would try to be the man of the house when his dad was off on a sailing trip. John was gone for months at times, and Mary would miss him, so George tried to cheer her up."

"How did he do that?" Megan asked.

Billy shrugged. "Oh, he'd bring her little treats after school. Maybe look for some wildflowers or sea glass. When they thought it was near time for John to be home, they'd go up to widow's walk every day and look for him. Sometimes, they'd spot a ship and get excited before it got close enough for them to figure out it wasn't him."

"That sounds so sad," Megan said. "I never realized how lonely my great-grandmother must have been when he was gone."

Billy scratched his head. "I guess it all worked out okay. I don't remember exactly when he stopped sailing, but he was mostly done by the time I met George. I know he was a good father by the stories George told me. He said John would always bring back little gifts from his trips and make sure they spent a lot of time together." Billy paused and laughed to himself. "I guess that changed once George met Rose."

The three looked at the ocean for a few minutes, considering Billy's words. Megan reached over and squeezed Billy's hand again. "Thank you for sharing that. Hey, you think you could do me a favor? If I brought you a journal would you write down any other memories that come to mind? Nothing fancy, but I'd enjoy hearing about my family. You know, the things they did and talked about back then."

"I could try, but I'm not good at writing."

"That's okay, Billy. I'm looking for some memories."

"I still have some for now. I have less as each month goes by."

"I'd appreciate anything you could share," Megan said.

"I'll think about it." Billy nodded as he watched the ocean.

Megan hugged him. "Thank you, Billy. Well, I guess we'd better be on our way. It was great seeing you today."

"It sure was," Nick added as they stood up from the bench. Together they turned and helped Billy stand up. Nick held the mail as they made their way back to the lighthouse and helped Billy up the stairs and into the lightkeeper's apartment.

"You sure I can't do anything to make this more comfortable for you?" Megan asked as she looked around the room. "How are you cooking all your food?"

"I'm fine, and Tommy brings me chowder from the fisherman's wharf. Don't be worrying about me."

"Okay, if you're sure," Megan said as she resolved to speak to Tommy the next time she saw him.

"Now, you two get out of here and enjoy the day. I'm sure you got more important things to do than hanging around with an old man like me."

CHAPTER 12

"How did the treasure hunt work out for the kids?" Megan turned from the boardwalk railing and looked at Georgie. "Did everyone have fun?"

"Yes, I think so," Georgie said as the three women walked along the boardwalk. "It was a fun event. We had free face painting and dressed up as pirates. Each kid was given a compass, a spyglass, and a treasure map. Then they went off in groups and found the buried treasure we hid in the sand."

Megan chuckled. "That sounds great! What was the treasure?"

"We had a pirate chest filled with plastic gold coins and fake pearls, but then we handed out chocolate gold coins while they listened to pirate stories on the beach and drank birch beer in mugs."

"That does sound like fun," Amber said while looking out at the water as they walked.

"Here's an interesting twist of events. The guy who was scheduled to do some of the talks canceled at the last minute, so guess who they got to fill in?"

"No clue," Megan said as she looked at Georgie expectantly.

Georgie laughed. "None other than Doogie Portman. Can you believe it?"

"Oh, the surfer boy?" Megan teased. The women slowed down as they reached multiple food stands on the boardwalk.

"The smell of those zeppoles are driving me crazy tonight," Amber said.

"You don't do anything other than smell them so what's the difference?" Georgie smiled and lightly punched her friend in the arm.

"Oh, shut up," Amber countered. "Sometimes, you're such a jerk."

"Just kidding. Hey, zeppole ingredients include ricotta cheese so you can still count it as protein, right?"

"You guys want to split a sausage sandwich? I could use a cold bottle of water," Megan said as she scanned the menu boards.

"Okay, sausage sandwich and two zeppoles and we split it in three," Amber said as she veered toward one of the food stands.

Georgie looked at Megan and shrugged. "She obviously doesn't know anything about zeppoles. You can't buy less than six in that shop."

Megan giggled and followed Amber toward the food.

Ten minutes later, they were seated on a wooden bench, facing the ocean. The salty sea breeze flowed through their hair as they finished the sandwich they had divided between them. Megan drank her cold water and looked at the beach as the sun went down. Most of the swimmers, as well as the lifeguards, were gone. A few couples walked along the shore, and in the distance, someone walked with their dog.

Behind them, Megan heard music playing, balloons popping as well as the excited screams of kids on the rides. The enticing smell of waffle cones and popcorn assailed them as they rested. Megan took another sip from her bottle and turned to her friends. "Tell me more about the stories Doogie told the kids."

Georgie smiled. "He told them about treasure ships that sank off the coast of New Jersey. He was good and brought the discussion down to their level, but I think you would have enjoyed it as well."

Intrigued, Megan nodded thoughtfully. "Does he know the history of New Jersey well?"

"Believe me, he's like the unofficial authority of the New Jersey Shore. You know, it's not too late."

"For what?" Megan asked. Hearing a moan, they turned to watch Amber eat a zeppole.

"This tastes so good," Amber said, hands full of sugared powder. "I haven't had a zeppole in years."

"You're starting to worry me," Georgie said as she watched her friend. "Keep it up, and I'm going to take you for medical help. I don't care where you work, it's okay to eat."

"Believe me, I've been eating plenty," Amber said as she licked her fingers.

"You wouldn't know it by watching you. You're acting like it's your first visit to the boardwalk."

"Just enjoying myself, that's all." Amber took another zeppole out of a greased stained paper bag and handed it to Megan. "Here, there's another four zeppoles in there. Two for each of you."

Megan looked in the bag. "I gotta say, these smell pretty good." She took two zeppoles and passed the bag to Georgie. As Megan bit into her warm zeppole, she looked at her friend. "You never answered. It's not too late for what?"

Georgie looked up and blinked for a moment. "Oh, I was talking about Doogie."

"Okay, what about him?"

"I was saying it's not too late to hear his talk. I've got the schedule. He'll be filling in at the library, but then I'd expect you'd know all about the talks scheduled there since you're the new board chair for the foundation."

Megan screwed up her face. "I'm just getting all the information straight for the animal shelter. I'm trying to learn about all the charities, but it takes time." Megan paused to pop the remaining zeppole in her mouth.

"You're making that face," Amber said with a tilt to her head.

"What?" Megan asked.

"You're making that face. You know, the expression you have when you're holding back something you should be telling us." Amber turned to Georgie. "Look at her. Aren't I right?"

Georgie squinted as she studied her friend. She began to nod. "You know, I think you're right, Amber. She's got something on her mind."

"You guys are crazy," Megan said. "I don't know what you're talking about."

"Now I know I'm right," Amber said as she stood and placed her hands on her hips. "Out with it. You were talking about the charities and then suddenly zipped up. What's going on?"

Georgie crossed her arms, with raised eyebrows as she waited for Megan to spill.

"Okay, okay, already. I want to learn about the charities, so I can follow in Grandma Rose's footsteps as quickly as possible. Teddy wants me to spend time with Jonathan to learn about them, but I feel funny doing that."

"Oh, do tell," Georgie said urging her to continue.

Megan looked down at her feet for a minute before answering. "Well, he's so different than Nick."

"How so?" Amber asked. "What's he doing?"

"Nothing bad," Megan said forcefully. "But instead of meeting somewhere and going over the list of charities, he wants everything to be more, I don't know," Megan shook her head as she thought of the right words. "Romantic, I guess."

"Oh, really?" Georgie said with a smile.

"Well, we can't sit in the library and talk about the estate. Jonathan wants us to sit on the beach with a picnic basket of fruit and fine wine or instead of visiting a specific place, he'll want to have lunch in town."

"Maybe he likes to eat," Georgie said as she laughed.

"No, it's not that," Megan said as she stood up and used a napkin to wipe her hands. "We can't have a meeting about business without playing golf or horseback riding."

"Very interesting," Amber said. "Does Nick know about any of this?"

Megan shook her head. "I sure haven't said anything. He doesn't like Jonathan as it is, and he doesn't know about our meetings."

"So, what's the play?" Georgie asked. "Why do you think he's doing that?"

Megan shrugged. "I don't know. It's like he's trying too hard, you know what I mean?"

"I think I may have an idea," Amber said. "Is he trying too hard to romance you or too hard to remain your estate attorney?"

"Well, last time we were all together, he kissed me on the cheek right in front of Nick."

"Ouch, so what did Nick do?"

"He kissed me on the other cheek."

"That's one way to turn the other cheek," Georgie laughed. "Boys will be boys."

Megan threw her napkin at Georgie. "Oh, shut up. Anyway, we've gotten way off track. What did you want to tell me about Doogie Portman?"

"As I said, he's doing another talk about shipwrecks off the coast of New Jersey and the history of the area. You seemed interested in the subject, so I thought you might want to go. I'll go with you."

Megan nodded as the group walked onto the pier. They watched as excited beachgoers lined up for rides. Different colored lights flashed while cars whirled in circles and music played. "I'd love for you to go with me but I'm curious if you're going for the history lesson or if you may have another agenda here."

Georgie frowned at her friends. "I hear he's a nice guy and he's got a reputation for being a kick-ass surfer. I wouldn't mind getting to know him better."

"I'm sure," Megan said as she giggled. "But I want to hear that talk. Check your schedule and let me know when we're going."

"I'm in," Georgie said as she looked at Amber. "What about you? You want to come with us?"

"It depends when it is," Amber said. "Give me the date, and I'll let you know."

"Sunday, tomorrow night," Georgie said. "Now who wants to go on a roller coaster? C'mon, the last one on is a rotten egg."

CHAPTER 13

"We've got to get in there, Nick," Megan said as she watched him carry a box into the library.

"I'm working on it as fast as I can."

Megan pulled the dictionary off the shelf and pulled the bookshelf toward her. She looked back at Nick who was unwinding a thick electric cable. "Are you ready?"

"Getting there. I need to find an outlet." He walked around the library and found an electric outlet to support the heavy-duty extension cord he brought in. He then plugged a bright lamp into the extension and pulled it into the room. "I think that will be plenty of light for us."

Moving forward, the pair quickly surveyed the room. It was apparent each area held things which her great-grandfather must have considered treasures. Megan spent time looking at the small maritime area which held a spyglass, compass, ship bell, ship logs, shells, netting and a photo of a ship.

"I'll bet he had some very interesting adventures," Nick said as he stood beside her and slipped an arm around her shoulders.

"It sure looks like it. I hope I find a diary or log where they're recorded. I think the ship logs will only have travel information, but it'll be fun reading through them."

"I want to look at that treasure map," Megan said as she turned toward the safe. "I thought Nathan was going to explode. A hidden treasure doesn't make sense to me if he had this room. He would have had plenty of places to hide it in the house or this room. He wouldn't have left it buried somewhere." Megan pulled the safe door open and pulled out the treasure chest again. She gently removed the turtle and pulled out the piece of parchment. The two stared at it for a few minutes. "It's still a little too dark in here. I'll bring it outside with us and see if I can't see more details. I don't believe there would be buried treasure here."

"Well, maybe he didn't bury it, or maybe it was a treasure he already found and kept the map."

"Or it could be a map of some other treasure which was buried by someone else. Maybe my great-grandfather meant to go looking for it and never did."

"We'll never know, but the turtle is pretty neat."

"I agree with you there," Megan said as she turned to Nick. "Doogie Portman is giving a lecture at the library on shipwrecks off the coast of New Jersey. He's quite the historian about the subject. I was thinking of going to his lecture tomorrow to see if I could learn anything. I also wanted to ask the librarian if there was a local history section dedicated to Misty Point. If not, I'm going to propose we set one up and maybe a specific section about Misty Manor. I don't know. I'm thinking about it."

"Did you ever speak to Teddy?"

"I haven't heard from him yet. Jonathan said he would let him know, but I'm going to have to follow up with a phone call."

"Can I ask a question?"

"Sure," Megan said, steeling herself for whatever Nick had on his mind.

"When your grandmother died, you inherited Misty Manor, and I'm guessing whatever was connected to the estate, right?"

Knowing Nick was not aware of the two hundred million dollars, Megan kept her answer vague. "Yes, that's true."

"Then you own all of this, so am I wrong in assuming that Teddy and Jonathan work for you?"

Megan paused for a minute to consider Nick's words. "Well, yes, when you put it that way."

"Then why do you always have to have their approval? It's yours to do what you want with." Nick stood there with his hands splayed. "I don't get it."

"Nick, it's not that simple. Part of it has to do with the fact that as the attorney, Teddy must follow the directions left to him in my grandmother's will. Secondly, Misty Manor and the rest of the estate as well as the trusts and charities which were established have legal obligations. I think Rose wanted to make sure Teddy and Jonathan watch that I don't do anything stupid. I told Teddy when she died that I knew nothing of committees and board chair responsibilities. It's his job to guide me."

"Whatever. My point is if you want to be in a room in your house, you should be able to do what you want without having to worry about them. This room has nothing to do with trusts and charities."

Megan smiled and took Nick's hand. "You're right. Thank you. I know you're trying to look out for me and look where we are. Just you and me, retrieving a treasure map. So, let's take it and go. We can come back at some point and take our time going through everything." Megan stuffed the map and the turtle in her pocket.

"You got it. We need to secure this room. Anyone who knows about it can waltz in your library and open the door. As you said, we don't know if this stuff is worth anything or just sentimental."

"You're the police officer. I'll leave that particular problem to you," Megan said as she made her way toward the doorway. As she was getting ready to step into the library, she felt the hair on the back of her neck rise and she stopped.

Nick pulled up short behind her and almost knocked her over. Grabbing her arm, he whispered. "What's wrong? Why did you stop?"

"Something's not right. I don't know what's wrong, but things aren't right." Megan didn't move. "I don't hear Dudley. He should be at the door, but I don't hear him."

Nick pushed her to the side. "Okay, let me go first. You stay here for a minute. Don't move unless I call you."

Nick pulled a gun out of the rear waistband of his pants and walked forward. Megan's eyes widened. "You have a gun?"

Nick held his right arm behind him to push Megan to the side. "Shhh, stay down."

He walked to the doorway and stood sideways as he looked out into the library. Megan watched him, her anxiety making everything seem much worse than it was. The room fell into darkness when the light went out. She felt herself shake as she watched Nick walk through the doorway and disappear. Her stomach clenched as she waited for what seemed like forever for Nick to return. Suddenly, she heard yelling and Nick commanding someone not to move. She shrunk to the floor and continued to listen. After five frightening minutes, the light in the room went back on and Nick appeared at the doorway.

"Megan, come on out here." She looked up to see Nick standing there. His hands were empty. Shaking, she stood and walked toward the entrance. She paused when she got to the doorway and looked out. Seated in a chair in the middle of the room was Nathan Graham. He had his elbows on the table, and his hands were zip-tied in front of him. Megan's eyes opened wide in disbelief. "Nathan? What are you doing here?"

"He was standing in the middle of the room when I went out there," Nick said as nodded his head in Nathan's direction.

"How did he get into the house?" Megan asked in surprise.

"The door was wide open, so I walked in," Nathan said. "This is a hell of a way to treat someone you want to work with."

"Wide open? Where's Dudley?"

"How the hell should I know?" Nathan said, his face screwed up in anger. "I never saw the dog. Can you tell your friend to get these things off me?" Nathan held his hands up as Megan looked toward Nick.

"I wanted to make sure we understood what was happening here. You can press charges if you want." Nick waited for Megan to respond but she ran toward the foyer and looked out the open front door to see if she could find Dudley. She ran down the stairs and checked the weeds to the side of the house. Racing toward the ocean, she did not see him near the water line. Frowning, she returned to the wrap-around porch and began to walk around the house. On the side, she found Dudley eating the remains of a cheeseburger. He had ripped the paper it was wrapped in and was licking the remaining ketchup off his paw.

"Dudley," Megan called out.

The dog looked up and wagged his tail before he walked toward Megan. She knelt and petted him to make sure he was unharmed. "Dudley, how did you get out here and where did you get that cheese-burger?" Instantly, she was concerned the food was poisoned or drugged, but Dudley looked normal, so far.

Together they walked back to the front door and went inside. Dudley stopped at the door to the library. The hair on his back began to rise, and a small growl emanated from his throat. Megan grabbed him by the collar and directed the dog to the kitchen before she returned to the library.

"Nick, what's going on?"

"Not quite sure. I'm waiting for him to tell me," Nick said as he pointed to Nathan who still had his hands zip-tied in front on him.

Nathan held his hands up to Megan and raised his eyebrows. "I told you, I came back to see what was going on and I found the door open. I didn't see any dog, so I stepped inside. Next thing I know, Rambo comes out of the secret room and goes crazy on me."

Megan turned toward Nick. "What was he doing when you came out here?"

"He was standing in the middle of the room, but it was a room he had no right to be in."

"Nick, let him go. I don't want to press any charges," Megan said as she turned to Nathan. "But in light of everything that's happened here, I think we're putting the project on hold."

Megan watched as Nick pulled out a pocket knife, walked over and cut the zip-tie. Nathan shook his hands in an exaggerated motion. "Your boss is going to hear about this."

"Go ahead, try it," Nick said. "You were trespassing on private property without invitation or permission to enter this house."

Nick looked back at Megan in an appeal to stay where she was. He turned back as Nathan stood and shook out his arms. "The zip-tie wasn't on very tight. Your circulation is fine. C'mon, I'll walk you out. You're lucky the lady is nice." Nick walked over and guided Nathan toward the foyer. As they approached the front door, Megan crept forward far enough to hear Nick continue to give advice. "Please don't come back without calling and in the future, for your own safety, never walk into someone's house uninvited. We'll give you a call if we're ever interested in your services again."

Nathan screwed up his face and shot Nick a dirty look. Once he was on the porch, Nick slammed the front door and locked it. He turned back to Megan. "I'm telling you that guy is up to no good."

"Teddy recommended him, so I assume he's a good guy. Maybe he meant no harm. He's the one who noticed the discrepancy to begin with," Megan pointed out. "Without Nathan, we wouldn't have known there was a secret room."

Megan immediately turned when she heard barking from the rear of the house. She hurried to the kitchen to check on Dudley. She found him pacing in front of the table. He rushed forward when he saw her and immediately jumped up. Megan hugged his big head and knelt to scratch him behind the ears. "Dudley, what's going on here today?"

"Nathan must have scoped out the house, gave Dudley the cheeseburger and entered the house which means he wasn't just popping in. He was probably very ticked off to find we were already back in the room."

Megan shrugged. "I'm very surprised. What are we going to do?"

"I'll tell you what I'm going to do and it's for your safety. I'm putting in a security system."

"I had the locks changed a year ago," Megan said as she pointed toward the door.

Nick chuckled. "I know you changed the locks when you came back to Misty Point, but that's not enough. I'm talking security system. Alarm keypads with motion sensors on the doors and windows. We can put a sensor up to detect breaking glass. I'll put an app on your phone. You'll love it," Nick said getting excited. "Oh, and we'll get new locks too."

Megan frowned and looked at Nick before rolling her eyes.

"Hey, it's your house, and you can overrule me, but I think it's time you're a little more secure around here."

"This has been one hell of a Saturday. Before we get too excited, let's close the library, grab a beer and talk about it."

CHAPTER 14

The next evening, Megan met Georgie and Amber in the parking lot of the Misty Point Library. Georgie had called them to confirm the time and room for Doogie's talk. They agreed to meet in the parking lot sixty minutes before the lecture, so they had time to chat. "So, he's waiting at the house for the security company to come and install the stuff he ordered," Megan said as she shook her head.

"And you're paying for all this?" Amber asked, her eyes widened.

"Yes, I guess I am, it's my house," Megan said, knowing the cost would be a minimal expense compared to her budget for the house. "He's trying to protect me."

"I think it's a great idea," Georgie said as they walked up the steps of the library. "Ever since you've come back to town, there's a lot of interest in Misty Manor. Face it, Megan, you've got a large parcel of prime land on the Jersey Shore. Lord knows how much it's worth, but I'm sure Teddy has a good idea which is why he has Jonathan sticking to you like glue."

"Plus, there are a lot of weirdos who live at the beach every summer. Who knows what they do for money or to survive?" Amber said.

"I'm not as worried about the weirdos coming to my house as I am about the mayor," Megan said as they entered the library. The three women laughed as they approached the librarian's desk.

"Hi, we're here for the talk by Doogie Portman," Georgie said as she smiled. Amber elbowed Megan as they watched Georgie speak.

"Yes, of course. Doogie's drawn quite a crowd compared to our original speaker," the librarian said as Georgie's face fell. "You'll find everyone in the large community room."

"Thanks." Georgie turned to her friends and gestured them toward the room.

"You're looking a bit disappointed," Megan said as she watched her friend walk by her side. "The lecture didn't start yet, so I know it's not the material."

Georgie looked down with a silly grin.

"Georgie, what is it?"

She shrugged. "I don't know. I guess I was hoping we'd be able to get close and that'll never happen with a hundred people around." She looked up and smiled. "Don't mind me, it's nothing." Georgie turned abruptly and walked into the community room. She picked out the first available row with three open seats. Unfortunately, it was near the back of the room.

The women walked past the attendees who were already seated and finally reached their seats. Amber leaned forward and talked over Megan. "What's the topic of the talk again? I haven't seen this many people at a lecture for years, including the mandatory corporate talks."

Georgie laughed as she looked at her friend. "He's speaking about shipwrecks off the coast of New Jersey. If anyone knows anything about the Jersey Shore, shipwrecks, treasures and beach life, it's Doogie."

Amber squinted at her friend for a moment. "Are you sure about that?"

George sent her friend a dismissive wave and sat back in her metal folding chair. She looked around the room to see who was present.

"Well, I for one, am looking forward to it," Megan said as she smiled at her friends. Excitement rose in the crowd as Doogie walked into the room accompanied by library personnel and Mayor Andrew Davenport. The group paused at the front of the room and checked the crowd to make sure everyone was seated. After a few moments, the crowd settled as they watched the guest speaker at the front of the room. Eventually, the librarian went to the podium and waited for silence.

"Hello, how are you all tonight?" The crowd clapped and cheered, indicating they were in fine spirits and the librarian continued. "Welcome to the Misty Point Library. As you know, our scheduled speaker was not able to make it." A few groans came from the crowd. "Now quiet down. We are very fortunate that one of our own has agreed to step in and speak, but I gather most of you know that. Our topic is sunken treasure and shipwrecks off the Jersey Shore by one of our local prize-winning surfers. Please join me in welcoming Doogie Portman to the podium." The librarian began to clap as she turned toward Doogie. The crowd clapped loudly and yelled out.

Megan leaned toward Georgie. "People are nuts over this guy."

"He's very popular because of all the great surfing he's done, but he's also very handsome and a great guy. He does things on the beach like collect different types of shells and sea glass and then teaches the kids all about them."

"That's sweet," Megan said as Doogie approached the podium.

The crowd continued to clap and cheer until Doogie raised his hands to quiet the crowd. "Thanks, thank you very much. As you've heard, we're going to talk about shipwrecks. Can anyone take a guess how many ships have sunk in these local waters?" Various members of the crowd shouted answers of 200, 400 and 500 while Doogie laughed. He finally quieted them once again.

"Not even close. There have been over 4000 shipwrecks off the coast of New Jersey, and there may be a lot more which remain undiscovered. Some of them are well charted and a favorite place for divers to visit. Others are reported to be located but are partially buried with sand and ocean plant life and are not yet obvious to the outside world.

Recent replenishment after Superstorm Sandy yielded the discovery of two buried shipwreck sites. Divers are exploring all the time."

The women listened as Doogie talked about the most famous and deadliest shipwrecks. He also described what items each ship was carrying. "It was common practice for the riches on a ship, or a treasure chest in some cases, to be offloaded into an emergency long boat and brought to the closest shore. There, the crew would bury their treasure and make a map to remember where they left it. When the time was right, the crew would return to collect their booty. The treasure map was made with various symbols to indicate dangerous areas as well as an innocuous symbol for where the treasure was directly buried. The symbols were kept private by the crew, so the treasure couldn't be found if the map fell into the wrong hands."

Megan sat up straighter as she tried to listen to the speaker over the murmuring of the crowd. She turned to Georgie. "This is an interesting lecture, but I can't hear everything he's saying."

"Who knew a hundred people would show up?" Georgie asked. "But yes, he's a great lecturer. Very smart, too."

Amber leaned forward and rolled her eyes at Megan who chuckled when she saw her. They quieted down to listen to the rest of the lecture.

"Okay, so let's talk about sunken treasure," Doogie said. "We've all heard about it, dreamt about it and found it quite exciting. We have our treasure hunts each year for the kids." The crowd clapped and cheered. "I'd like to, and excuse me for a trite phrase, dive a little deeper into this topic." The crowd tittered at his joke. "From the records we have, it appears the first recorded shipwrecks off the coast of NJ were in the early 1700's, and they've continued through recent times."

Doogie turned around and pulled a dry erase marker off a shelf behind him. "I'd like to make a list of some of the most common treasures you'd find on one of those ships. What do you think they were?" As the crowd yelled out suggestions, Doogie wrote on the whiteboard. After a few minutes, Doogie had a list which included gold, diamonds, doubloons, pearls, ivory and more. He put the marker down and picked up another color. "Okay, the first item on our list is gold. And yes, there has been gold treasure found in sunken ships, but what was considered more common in the day was coal." He wrote the word coal next to gold and turned back to the crowd. "Next we have diamonds. The diamonds which were found must have been tucked into a treasure chest because the ocean would have covered those beauties within minutes." He turned to the board and next to diamonds he wrote, lumber. "Lumber was a commodity in the past and a common cargo on ships. To save time, I'm going to list for you other common cargo items. They include whiskey, corn, clams, fish oil, coconuts, oranges, china and cotton among other things. So, you see we romanticize the thought of a ship on the high seas and the cargo it held. Cargo, and therefore, sunken treasure, was much more pragmatic than believed." Doogie put the marker down on the shelf and turned back to the crowd. "Okay, does anyone have questions?"

Megan turned to Georgie. "He's very good. Thank you for inviting me tonight. The lecture was very interesting."

"My pleasure," Georgie said with a slight frown. "I wish we could've gotten a little closer."

Megan reached out and patted Georgie's arm. "Things will work out if they're meant to."

"I never thought I'd see the day when Georgie was pining over someone," Amber whispered to Megan.

The three women turned and joined the crowd leaving the community room. A small group of people had gathered around Doogie to ask specific questions. As they neared the main library, Megan steered them toward the reading room. "Come with me for a minute, I'd like to check on something." She led them to the quiet area, where large tables were set up for reading or work, with comfortable lounging chairs placed around the edges of the room. Each table had electric outlets placed nearby to charge equipment or phones.

"Looks great, doesn't it?"

Megan turned as the librarian appeared at her elbow. "It's very welcoming."

"I want to personally thank you once again for advocating for the library. The grant from your foundation allowed us to put in four new public computers, great tables and chairs, and order new books and journals, as well as paying the electric bill. I'm thrilled you're keeping literacy in the forefront."

"You're most welcome," Megan said. "Education unlocks portals to whole new worlds. I want everyone to know it's okay to get off their phones and read for pleasure, as well as business or school."

"Well, you've helped us tremendously, and I'm glad you feel that way," she said with a large grin. "My name is Lindsey."

A door behind them opened, and a few library volunteers walked out followed by Doogie. They waited for the small group to approach. The librarian reached out and shook Doogie's hand. "Thank you so much for filling in for us. Everyone loves to hear you speak."

"You're very welcome," he said as he looked at the group with a smile.

"We're looking at the new quiet room," Lindsay said. "Courtesy of the Stanford Grant. Do you know Megan Stanford? She's Rose's granddaughter and the new owner of Misty Manor."

"Yes, we met the other day," Doogie said as he shook her hand. He then smiled at Amber and Georgie as Lindsey walked to the other side of the library to help someone.

"I'm glad we bumped into each other," Doogie said as he turned to Megan. "I wanted a chance to talk to you about an environmental issue. I want to start a campaign to prohibit plastic on the beach and thought we could toss around ideas. Some of the business owners won't be happy if they have to serve drinks in different containers, but we have to protect the ocean and the beach."

Megan paused for a moment and nodded. "I've heard a lot about the effect of plastic on our world, so it's good to start talking about it. I'd like to hear your ideas."

"Great," Doogie said. "Thanks for considering it."

"As a matter of fact, I'm wondering if you could help me with another issue as well," Megan said. "Are you free to come to Misty Manor for dinner tomorrow evening?"

"Yeah, of course. That would be great," Doogie said.

Megan turned to Georgie and Amber. "Are you two free to come for dinner? Perhaps Tommy is available, and I'll invite Nick as well."

The two women nodded. "Sure, we'd love to come."

"What's on the menu?" Georgie teased. "Pizza?"

Megan shook her head. "No, I'll ask Marie to make us a nice dinner." She turned to Doogie. "You're our guest of honor. What would you like?"

"Oh, I don't know. The menu is completely up to you," Doogie said with a shrug.

"Okay, I'll talk to Marie and then decide. Let's plan on having pre-dinner drinks at 7:00 p.m. and then we'll have Marie serve around 7:30 p.m. in the dining room."

"I take it shorts and t-shirts are out?" Amber teased as she elbowed Georgie.

Megan sighed as she looked at her friends. "You can wear whatever you want, but it may be nice if you dressed up a bit."

"Okay, if we have to," Amber said with a sarcastic smile.

"Great, then it's a date for tomorrow night," Megan said as she turned to Doogie. "We'll see you then?"

"Wouldn't miss it for the world," he said. "Goodnight."

"Goodnight," the women sang out as he walked away. A few minutes later, they walked out to their car as Georgie hissed. "Are you out of your mind?"

Megan laughed as she got into her car. "See you tomorrow night, ladies. Georgie, you can thank me later."

CHAPTER 15

"What are we doing?" Nick asked as he listened to Megan speak.

"We're having dinner with Doogie Portman and the gang," Megan said as she sat down on the top step of the porch. While she spoke, she watched Dudley run on the beach under the moonlight. The waves were loud as they pounded the shore and the evening breeze was warm and fragrant with salt air. Megan relaxed as she rested and suddenly wished she had a hammock she could lie on when she spent time on the porch. Falling asleep on the beach seemed like a great end to a stressful day.

"And why are we doing this?" Nick asked, snapping Megan back to the present.

Megan sighed as she pushed the phone closer to her ear. "From what everyone is saying, Doogie is one of the best Jersey Shore historians. I want to ask him if he has any information on Misty Manor. He must have heard something about the place. Nathan had a good idea when he suggested we start a historical section in the library on Misty Manor and the Stanford family."

"Are you sure you don't have to ask Jonathan permission?"

"Nick, please don't be sarcastic. You're the one who said they work for me, so I made an independent decision. Please be here by 6:00 p.m. Everyone else will be here by 7:00 p.m."

Dudley ran up the porch stairs and leaned against Megan as he panted in her ear. She scratched his head and hugged him to her.

"Okay, I get off shift around 5:00 p.m. so I'll have to run home and change, but I'll be there as soon as I can."

"Thank you," Megan said to soothe him. "Dress nice. We're going to eat in the formal dining room and then we'll probably go out on the porch afterward."

"Yes, ma'am," Nick said as he received instructions.

"Nick, don't be like that," Megan said. "I'm trying to figure everything out."

"I know, I'm sorry. Work was frustrating today. The weekend always brings a lot of hysterics to the beach. Everyone wants to drink, smoke and drop their trash on the beach if they're not stealing something from their neighbor's blanket."

"I'm sorry to hear that," Megan said. "Georgie has told me some interesting stories as well."

"To be honest, I used to love summer. The excitement was palpable as the beach, and the town came to life, but now that I'm a permanent officer, I can't wait for September to roll around, so everyone goes home."

"Hopefully, tomorrow will be a better day," Megan said as she yawned into the phone. "Let me go so we can both get some rest."

"You got it, Buttercup," Nick said as he yawned himself.

"You haven't called me that since high school," Megan said as she giggled into the phone.

"Old habits die hard. Get inside the house. I'm staying on the phone until I know the door is locked and you're safe," Nick said. "Go ahead, get going."

Megan groaned. "It's so nice out here. I could fall asleep on the porch."

"Maybe someday when I'm with you, but not tonight."

"Okay, I'm moving," Megan said as she stood up and made her way into Misty Manor. After calling the dog, she said, "Okay, we're inside."

"Fine, now activate the new security system. I used the code you wanted," Nick said as he waited for her to push the buttons.

Megan looked at the new panel and punched numbers into the keypad. When she was finished, the green button lit up. "I think I did it, Nick."

"Did the button on the top right-hand corner turn green?"

"It sure did," Megan said, pleased with herself.

"Okay, now you can go to bed."

"Thanks, Dad," Megan laughed. "I'll talk to you in the morning."

"Goodnight, sweet dreams."

"Goodnight," Megan whispered as she hung up the phone. She walked through the first floor of the Grand Victorian home. After making sure the cat and the dog were fed for the night, she turned down all but the security lights. She made her way up the grand staircase, followed by the pets until she reached her room on the third floor. She turned the old-fashioned, round, brass doorknob to open the door. She quickly changed, opened her windows and turned off the lights. Once again, she could hear the surf pound the shore and smell the sweet salty air as it flowed through her window. Crawling into bed, Megan fell asleep within seconds as the curtains floated in the breeze. She didn't see the man on the beach, staring up at her window before he flicked his lit cigarette in the ocean.

CHAPTER 16

"*L*et me help you," Megan said as she rushed over to Marie.

"It's a good thing you called me last night," Marie said as she handed over a grocery bag and nudged the front door closed with her right foot. "I was able to get to the market early and found everything I was looking for."

"Goodness," Megan said as she placed the bags on the table. "What are you planning to make tonight?"

"Well, you said you wanted a nice seafood dinner, but nothing too fancy."

"Yes, so what did you come up with?" Megan eagerly watched as Marie unloaded the contents of the shopping bags onto the table.

"Well, I saw a few new recipes online, so I thought I would start by serving lobster rolls and crab cakes."

"That sounds delicious," Megan said. "What if someone doesn't like fish?"

Marie made a face and shrugged. "Stuffed mushrooms with sweet sausage."

Megan's stomach growled. "You're going all out. I admit I want to have a nice dinner, but I don't want you to exhaust yourself."

Marie put something in the freezer, closed the door and turned back to the table. "To be honest, I enjoy cooking very much, and I'm excited you finally have some decent company I can cook a nice meal for. I hope this works out and we start entertaining more often."

Megan laughed. "Let's not get too excited. I still have an aversion to people in general."

"We can start with your friends and go on from there," Marie said as she wagged a finger in Megan's direction. "It'll be good for you not to be isolated in this gorgeous, large house."

"I'll keep that in mind. What about the main course?"

Standing with one fist on her cocked hip, Marie looked at Megan. "That's what I wanted to talk to you about. At first, I thought you and your friends would want something like beer battered fish and chips, but I wanted to make something a little nicer. I got a great price on large jumbo shrimp so I can make jambalaya or a traditional garlic shrimp scampi." Marie raised her hand toward Megan and said, "Before you even ask, I'm making chicken francese for those who don't eat fish." Marie walked over to the counter and emptied another bag. "Can you imagine people living near the beach and not enjoying fish?" She pulled several bottles of wine from the bag. "Garlic loves a nice sauvignon blanc, and so does chicken francese, so I bought a couple of bottles and thought it would make a nice wine choice during dinner."

Megan took the bottle as it was handed to her. "Okay, now I'm starving, and I can't wait to eat. I'm going to have some of everything, but that's a lot of cooking. Are you sure it's not asking too much for you to do all of this?"

Marie smirked at Megan's concern. "Cooking for six people? That's not even a party by my count, but I'm so excited to have someone to cook for, I'm going to start right away. We'll have nice leftovers for a day or so as well."

"Yes, it sounds like we will," Megan agreed.

"You didn't ask about dessert, but I'll tell you anyway. I'm making an amaretto cake and I'll serve it with rich espresso coffee. Beyond that, you kids can drink whatever you want."

"Drink? After that meal, I'm going to be sound asleep," Megan teased. "And so will you from cooking all day."

"Yes, but I'll be happy. By the way, I thought I'd sleep here so I can take my time with dishes and cleaning up."

"Marie, you have a permanent room here. You can stay or go home whenever you want, and you don't have to ask my permission. I appreciate all the help with the pets as well. Dudley and Smokey love you as much as I do and don't tell me they're spoiled, because you've spoiled them as much as I have."

"They don't crawl into my bed at night," Marie said with a pointed look at Megan.

Dudley was now at Megan's side, leaning against her leg with wounded eyes, looking up at her which made Megan laugh. "I was so tired last night I fell asleep within minutes. I wasn't aware they were on the bed until I woke up this morning with Dudley almost on top of me."

Marie clucked as she shook her head. "That's fine. What about all the other nights? It doesn't matter. I'll keep them in the kitchen with me during dinner."

Megan walked over and hugged Marie around the shoulders. "I appreciate all you do."

Marie feigned annoyance and brushed her away. "Go away, so I can start cooking."

Laughing, Megan walked out of the kitchen. "How about I check the dining room and set the table for dinner?"

"Sounds like a good idea," Marie said as she tied a flowery apron around her waist.

CHAPTER 17

*A*fter an hour of work, Megan stepped back to admire the dining room. She had cleaned the dining room table until it sparkled. As a child, she had sat at this table many times but never actually thought about it. The original dining room table must have been replaced several times over the hundred years Misty Manor had been in existence. However, Megan didn't remember any other table except for the one she saw before her now.

The table looked elegant. Megan had gone through her grandmother's sideboard and pulled out the silver candlestick holders, lace tablecloth and linen place settings. The more she went through the items stored there, the more excited she was about having a dinner party. She remembered using the fancy settings at holidays when she was young, but at some point, that had stopped between her parent's fights and grandmother's illness.

Megan took a moment to look at the gorgeous portrait of her grandmother in the middle of the dining room wall. In the portrait, her grandmother was young and smiling while standing on the lawn with the ocean in the background. Her dark hair was swept up with a beautiful comb, and she was wearing an Edwardian white tea party dress. She looked so happy and carefree, and Megan realized how her grandmother's life must have changed since then.

Returning to the task at hand, Megan removed the tarnish from the candlestick holders and then found beautiful ivory candles to place in them for dinner. The silverware was easier to clean and set. As she continued to dig through the sideboard, she found some of her grandmother's china platters and soup tureen. She carried them all into the kitchen and left them with Marie to use as she saw fit for dinner. Once dinner was over, Megan wanted to spend time reorganizing the entire sideboard. Her grandmother's things were so beautiful it was a shame to keep them locked away. As a final touch, she placed wine glasses and water goblets in front of each place setting.

After stepping back for one last review of the dining room, Megan went upstairs to pick out her clothing. She planned to shower and apply her makeup but had time to kill. She sat on her bed, pulled out her large iPad and started surfing the net. Dudley and Smokey must have decided to stay with Marie in the kitchen after they got a whiff of the dinner she was preparing.

Megan wanted to hear more about shipwrecks off the coast of New Jersey and planned to ask Doogie more questions, but she wanted to prepare in advance. If her great-grandfather's map did lead to a real treasure, it was possible it was collected from a shipwreck around the turn of the century.

Megan started with keywords such as shipwrecks, sea captains, pirate treasure and found a lot of generic material. She tried to search for a history of New Jersey shipwrecks and found a few great references, but when she googled her great-grandfather, no specific information surfaced.

Turning off the iPad, she pulled out the treasure map and unfolded it on the bed. Once again, she studied the pattern of symbols and lines, but nothing made sense. She pulled out her cell phone and snapped a couple of photos of parts of the map. One of the symbols looked like a lighthouse and next to it was a line, but after several minutes she found no definitive pattern. Frustrated, she folded the map and hid it in her favorite place which was a ceramic bible placed inside the lower vent of her bedroom. Earlier, she had placed the turtle on her dresser, where it currently sat.

Finally, she collected her bath things, went across the hall and took her shower. She spent extra time with her makeup and long brown hair. She chose an off the shoulder, gauzy peach dress with sandals. Her jewelry for that evening was from her grandmother's collection which she had cleaned and separated into a new holder. Some of the antique pieces were exquisite, and she chose a chain with a gold starfish which was set off beautifully by the peach dress.

For the first time in years, she had decent color to her face. In the past, she always used sunscreen and never spent hours in the sun but living near the beach gave her a healthier glow than the pasty, pale wan she had sported while living in Detroit. With one final glance in the mirror, she grabbed her cell phone and ran downstairs to wait for Nick.

CHAPTER 18

egan found Dudley and Smokey in the kitchen, standing at Marie's feet.

"Dinner smells fantastic," Megan said as she surveyed the pots and pans on the stove.

"Don't get too excited. We have a little time yet before everything is ready. I added an ice bucket and a few other things to your table, but I think we're mostly set for dinner."

"Thank you for helping me with my friends. I thought it would be nice to offer dinner to Doogie before I pummel him with questions."

"It's nice to see you're smiling for a change," Marie said. "Well worth a good meal and pleasant company."

Megan didn't have a chance to respond before the doorbell rang. "It's probably Nick, so I'll get the door." Dudley jumped up and raced to the foyer ahead of her. He barked and wagged his tail as he waited for Megan to reach the door.

"Dudley, don't jump when Nick comes in. We don't want to mess his clothes." Dudley looked at her for several seconds before he barked as if he was asking her what she was waiting for. Megan opened the door and invited Nick in. He placed his hand, palm down toward the dog so he wouldn't jump and then scratched Dudley behind the ears.

It was obvious the dog loved Nick. Silently stalking down the foyer hall, Megan noted Smokey near the wall. He preferred to stay in the shadows, watch the activities and plan his next strike.

"Hey, you're looking pretty good," Nick said as he leaned over and kissed Megan.

When she pulled back, she said, "You clean up pretty well yourself." He was wearing pressed tan khaki pants with a blue polo shirt which set off his eyes. "You look very nice, Nick."

"As opposed to my usual self," Nick laughed as he watched her.

"No, as opposed to being in your uniform although that fits you well, too."

"I see you've noticed," Nick teased.

"Enough of that, I was complimenting you."

"Well, thank you very much," Nick said as he kissed her on the nose. "Before we go anywhere and speaking as a cop, do you understand how to use the security system?"

"I don't know. I think so, I did it the one time, but I'm not sure I know everything," Megan said with a shrug.

"We're not going anywhere until I run through it with you." He dragged her to the keypad and showed her how to alarm the system, set the sensors and most importantly, check the cameras when the alarm went off. "Think you have it now?"

Megan nodded her head. "I think so. I'll give it a go, but I'll let you know if I get stuck."

"Good, I'll feel better if I know you're secure in this house."

"Thank you for taking care of me, Nick. That's very sweet of you."

"As long as you say that again when you get the bill," Nick laughed.

"Very funny. Let's go on the deck and wait for everyone," Megan said as she opened the door. They stepped outside and moved to the wide end of the porch. Wicker chairs surrounded a table which held a cold pitcher of martinis. A tray with glasses sat on the edge of the table and waited for the dinner guests to arrive.

"Hey, this looks marvelous," Nick said as he checked the porch.

"Thanks, I think I like the idea of entertaining friends. Marie is all about it and wants me to do it more often."

"I imagine you'll have more company as you restore Misty Manor. It's a beautiful home in a great location owned by a gorgeous girl. What else can you ask for?"

Megan laughed. "I can probably find a lot to ask for. In the meantime, I want to tell you about what's going on. I invited Doogie to ask him more questions about the history of the Jersey Shore. I'm hoping he's researched something about my great-grandfather and the town of Misty Point."

"We can only ask him," Nick said.

"He wanted to speak to me anyway about an environmental cause he's championing so maybe we can help each other."

"Let's hope so. Was there any history about the town in the library?"

"I never got a chance to ask the librarian. Everyone was talking and asking for things after Doogie's lecture, so I didn't press her on it, but I can always go back."

"If not the library, the town must have public records or deeds on the land and building permits."

"Yes, I'll have to check with them as well," Megan said as she stood against the porch rail looking toward the ocean.

"Or you could ask your good friend, Jonathan, what his father, Teddy, has on file about the estate."

"Nick, please don't get snarky," Megan said as she spied Amber, Tommy and Georgie exiting the boardwalk via the ramp. "Here comes the gang."

Nick looked toward the ocean. "There they are. I guess Doogie's coming on his own."

"Yes, but I'm pairing him up with Georgie as long as she doesn't get so nervous she does something dumb."

"Matchmaking? From what I hear that blows up in the matchmaker's face a good percentage of the time."

"All I'm doing is serving dinner. Anything else that happens is up to hormones and mother nature."

Nick laughed as their friends climbed the stairs to Misty Manor. Megan called for them to walk down to the end of the porch. "Hey guys, you look great." Always the fashion plate, Amber was in a Lily Pulitzer summer dress with matching sandals and purse. Tommy looked very nice in slate grey dress pants paired with a maroon polo shirt.

Megan turned to Georgie. "Is that a Ted Baker? I don't think I've ever seen you in a dress. Usually, you're wearing a standard lifeguard bathing suit or jeans, but you look gorgeous. You've got legs to die for in that dress." Georgie spun and showed off the cold shoulder scalloped dress with sandals. "I'm serious. You're perfect for that dress."

"Drop dead, gorgeous," a voice said behind them. They turned to see Doogie Portman standing behind them. He looked great in a Patagonia Pataloaha shirt, dark slacks, and designer boat deck shoes with no socks.

"Thank you," Georgie said. "Amber helped me pick it out."

Nick walked over to the white wicker table. "Hey, I've got a cold pitcher of martinis here if anyone is interested.

"I'm in," Megan said as the group moved closer to the beverage table. Nick expertly poured the martinis in glasses and handed them to the crowd. They sipped their drinks while sharing small talk about the town. At one point, Doogie was standing at the porch railing, looking toward the ocean. The day was perfect. Beautiful blue-green waves rushed to the shore, the wind was warm and scented but not intrusive on their party, the temperature had dropped enough to make everyone comfortable and relaxed. A day full of exercise and sun, combined with liquor relaxed everyone.

"You've got a gorgeous place here," Doogie said as he turned to Megan. "There must be a dozen real estate investors offering large sums of money to own Misty Manor. The location, the house, and the lighthouse make it a prime piece of land."

Megan paused for a few seconds. "You know, now that you mention it, I've never had an offer or even a query as to whether the house is for sale. Don't get me wrong, I'd never sell Misty Manor now that it's mine. I went through quite an ordeal with my father last year. He assumed he would inherit after my grandmother died and he had a developer here within hours. A developer. Can you imagine? The guy wanted to knock the house down and build condos or something."

"How did you get rid of him?" Doogie asked as he finished his drink.

Megan paled. "That's a long story, but my father didn't inherit the estate, so he had no right to sell it. Let's leave it at that."

"I get it, but I can't believe no one has approached you since."

"Maybe they know I'm not interested," Megan shrugged.

Doogie shook his head. "I doubt it. If there's someone who has his eye on the place, he'll keep renewing his offer from time to time, in case you change your mind."

"No one has approached me," Megan said with a slight frown.

"I'll bet they're going straight to your attorney," Doogie said with a shrug.

"Anyone want another round?" Nick asked. "There's plenty here as long as you don't plan to drive away." He split the remains of the pitcher with the group on the deck while they continued to chat.

"So, Tommy, what's going on with the band?" Megan asked.

Tommy swallowed his last bit of martini. "I'm glad you asked. You're never going to believe this because I don't believe it myself, but we're going to open for another band at the PNC Bank Arts Center. It's one of the smaller shows, but the opening act had to cancel at the last minute. The organizer asked around and was given my name, so they called, and we hammered it out." Amber beamed behind Tommy as he delivered his news.

"That's incredible," Megan said with a smile. "You're famous!"

"I'm sure he will be soon," Amber said as she stroked his arm. "And guess what? Tommy said I could be backstage during the show."

"Although you're not going to see or hear much there, so you should go out front when it starts and sneak back near the end," Tommy said as put his arm around her. "We'll talk more about it later on."

"When's the show?" Nick asked walking over to the crowd.

"Two weeks," Tommy said. "I'm getting a bunch of tickets so don't plan anything else. I want you all to come and sit with Amber in the front row."

"Sounds exciting," Megan said as she looked at Nick. "We would love to come."

"Good, I'll get the tickets to you all by next week."

The group turned when Marie opened the front door and rang a small school bell. "I hate to break things up here, but the food is ready, and it's best to serve at a certain temperature."

Marie walked to the end of the porch and started collecting the glasses and pitcher as the group walked indoors. Nick and Megan helped Marie to make sure everything was brought inside to the kitchen. She paused to give Dudley and Smokey a nice long scratch behind the ears and assured them she would spend time with them later, but they'd have to stay in the kitchen for now.

Back in the foyer, Megan led her guests into the dining room and showed them where to sit, ensuring that Doogie and Georgie would be seated on one side of the table, while Amber and Tommy were on the other. As Georgie walked past her, she opened her eyes wide and gave a funny smirk which showed her anxiety. Megan chuckled and patted her on the arm.

When the group was settled and had arranged their napkins, Marie rolled in a cart with the soup tureen. Although she hadn't mentioned it, she had managed to make clam chowder and served it with oyster crackers from the cart.

While they ate their soup, Marie brought in several platters with the appetizers of lobster rolls and crab cakes. A short time later she brought out the shrimp scampi and chicken francese. Nick poured the wine which Marie had opened before dinner to let it breathe.

Georgie attempted to pick up her fork and then awkwardly dropped it between her and Doogie. He reached down and plucked it off the floor before wiping it and handing it back to her. "Looks like there's plenty of silverware on the table, but there's always the five-second rule." She turned red, but his warm smile made her blush even more.

While laughing and chatting, the group dug in and had their

dinner. Eventually, Tommy sat back and sighed. He wiped his hands on his napkin and dropped it on the table. "I don't think I've ever had a meal like this."

"Marie is a wonderful cook," Megan said as she placed her fork across her plate.

"Everything was delicious," Amber said as she placed another shrimp in her mouth. Megan was pleased that Amber had a good appetite and didn't want to spoil it by teasing her for not eating as much as she should.

"I'm more than full," Nick said as he tried one more mouthful of dinner.

"Well, save a little room," Megan said. "Marie made an almond amaretto cake for dessert."

The group collectively moaned as Megan stood and started collecting things from the table. Marie ran in with the cart and shooed her back to her seat while she cleared the table. She explained that she would be back in a moment with coffee, tea, and cake.

"I don't know if I can eat anything else," Amber said as she backed a few inches away from the table. Everyone agreed with her but knew they would have coffee, cake and whatever else Marie brought into the room.

"This has been such a beautiful meal, I feel guilty bringing up my private agenda, but I did want to talk to you about an environmental issue if you have a few minutes," Doogie said to Megan.

She smiled at him. "It does appear we have some time but don't feel bad because I have an agenda for you." She looked around at the group. "We can talk freely in front of everyone here."

Doogie surveyed the group, cleared his throat and began. "I've been told the grant or charities your grandmother started are wonderful to the community, and I was wondering if there was any way I could get you or the lawyer who's overseeing the foundation to consider helping me raise awareness and money to get plastic off the beach. We've been working on a ban for smoking on the beach, and now I'd like to add plastic and other trash. Of course, the local vendors won't be happy as they'd have to buy different straws and beverage containers, but if we can make it law, we'd have a cleaner environment and attract more families. Their business may not suffer."

"I for one would be thrilled if we could keep the beach clean," Georgie said. "The lifeguards are constantly picking up trash at the end of the day. I don't understand why people can't be responsible enough to clean their areas."

"I know, right?" Doogie said as he realized Georgie would be a strong ally for him. "Some tourists are slobs. How would they like it, if people showed up in their backyard and left trash all over their lawn?"

"They would scream bloody murder," Georgie said as the two locked in on each other.

Megan looked at Nick and saw his lips twitch, but he was able to stifle his reaction.

After a moment, Megan asked, "Do we use a beach sweeper in the morning?"

Doogie paused before he spoke. "The town has a beach rake which is towed by a tractor trailer, but it's old. The operator has to go out at 6:00 a.m. so he can get the beach clean before the sun worshipers come out for the day."

"How much is a new beach rake?" Megan asked.

"A large one is approximately $5,000.00," Doogie said. "There are smaller models for less money, but they cover smaller areas. The big rake can cover up to nine acres in an hour with a seven-foot width."

"You certainly know your beach rakes," Megan teased.

"Well, it would be great to have a newer, larger model so we could clean more of the beach at a faster rate, but it would be best to ban the garbage from the beach to begin with," Doogie said. "Of course, cleaning the beach is officially a town problem, but at times they are less than effective, and the mayor won't give me the time of day."

"No kidding?" Megan said as she looked at her friends for support. "I think it's a great idea." The group agreed and suggested other ways the beaches could be kept clean. "The only issue is I'm being mentored about the foundation by the estate attorney, which isn't a problem," she quickly put in. "But I need to run this by him or his son because I don't have complete control over the finances."

"That's okay," Doogie said. "I'd appreciate anything you could do to help us."

"It's a deal. I'll let you know as soon as I talk to Teddy."

"So, you said you had questions for me?" Doogie prompted Megan as they waited for dessert.

"Yes, I do," Megan said somewhat sheepishly. "This may seem strange, but I'm told you're one of the best Jersey Shore historians, so I wanted to ask you if you'd ever heard anything about my family, my great-grandfather specifically or Misty Manor or the origin of Misty Point."

Doogie picked up his water glass and took a deep drink. "Now that is an interesting question."

"I know it sounds strange since it's my family, but someone recently asked me if the library or I had a historical archive of my family or the town. I only know what my grandmother told me. My parents fought a lot, so there weren't many heartfelt family moments while I was growing up. I recently learned some of the history of Misty Manor when I returned last year and found a body in one of the cabins out back, but I don't know a lot about my family before that."

Megan nervously picked up her water glass and gulped down half the content.

"One thing you could do is go to town hall," Doogie said as he chuckled. "I understand your great-grandfather built Misty Manor before there was a town, but a copy of the deed has to be recorded and archived somewhere. You can start there and then build. I don't have any specific tidbits about your family, but I can check a source I have for sea captains and see if he's listed there. It's funny, but I never thought to look him up. What was his full name?"

Megan smiled as she offered the information. "His name was John Anthony Stanford. He was born somewhere around 1880. I believe he was gifted the land around 1910. He married my great-grandmother Mary, and he had Misty Manor built as her wedding gift. The house has stayed in the family, generation after generation, and will continue to do so." Megan blushed. "Of course, I would need to have a few children first."

"I'll be happy to help you out with that," Nick said. The group laughed as Megan turned a deep shade of red.

"Thank you, I'll let you know if I'll be in need of your services," Megan replied as the laughter escalated.

Marie walked into the dining room pushing the cart in front of her. She had a coffee carafe, and the delicious aroma of strong coffee filled the room. Once she placed the delicate cups, coffee, sugar, and cream on the table, she added a decadent almond amaretto layer cake. She expertly sliced the cake, plated several pieces and passed them around the table. She then reached down to the next shelf on the cart and brought up bottles of Kahlua, Amaretto, and Frangelico. She placed them on the table with the appropriate glasses. "In case anyone wants a bit of something to go with the cake."

"Marie, this is the best dinner I've had in a long time," Tommy said. "I'm going to have to find a way to come back often."

Marie frowned and placed her hand on her hip. "You know you can eat my cooking anytime you want, Tommy, but I'm sure Miss Megan would offer even more if you helped out with some of the chores around here."

"Aww, Marie, I help Uncle Billy as much as I can, but the band is starting to get busy, and I still have to work at the marina, too."

"That's fine, but don't forget about us. I'm packing up some food for your Uncle Billy. When you're done here, you and Amber can take it over to the lighthouse for me. That would save me a trip and cheer your uncle up a bit."

Tommy nodded. "Yes, ma'am."

Megan felt awkward and jumped in. "Do you want Nick and I to walk it over?"

Tommy shook his head. "No, I want to check in on him anyway, so this will work out fine."

"Thank you," Marie said with a small smile and a nod.

"The meal was divine," Megan said as she thanked her, and the rest of the guests joined in. "I don't think I can move."

"Well, you sit there and digest," Marie said as she smiled while they finished their cake and sipped coffee.

"How about if we help you clear the dishes?" Megan asked as she started to rise from her chair.

"Don't you dare," Marie said as she pushed her back down in the chair. "You relax with your friends, and I'll take care of the table. That's my business, none of yours."

"Are you sure?"

"Absolutely," Marie said. "I'll be back later. Enjoy your dessert."

The group watched her leave the room and once again remarked on how wonderful dinner was.

"Megan, I was wondering," Doogie said. "Have you found any logs or diaries or maps from your great-grandfather? Most sea captains were very specific record keepers."

"I haven't started going through my family's things or explored the house yet, but perhaps I'll find something then."

"Well if you do, start keeping notes. You should write a historical summary of your family. I'm sure many people around here would buy a book about the Stanford family especially if there are a few well-kept secrets," Doogie said with a chuckle.

Megan opened her eyes wide. "Why do you say that? Do you know of any?"

"No, not at all," Doogie said as he wiped his mouth. "But most families have a few interesting things to talk about after four generations."

"I would buy it, for sure," Amber said.

"Me too," Georgie added. "Just to make sure I'm not in it."

"Hey, knock it off you two," Megan said as she laughed. "Come to think of it, there are a few good stories I could add." Megan shot them a pointed look.

Amber made a motion as if she were zipping her lip and then poured herself a small amount of Amaretto. Tommy asked for some as well. The rest of the group deferred.

Megan seemed to debate with herself for a few minutes. Eventually, she held her cell phone and brought up a photo. She caught

Doogie's attention and showed him the photo. "This is something I found the other day. It's only a piece of something. Does it make any sense to you?"

Nick looked at her with eyebrows raised. She hadn't told him she had a photo of only a small portion of the treasure map.

Doogie studied the photo before him. "The paper looks old, that's for sure."

"What about that house there with the wavy lines," Megan asked as she pointed to the symbol in the photo.

Doogie scratched his chin. "I'm not sure, but in the "old" days, that may have been a symbol they would've used to indicate a lighthouse. They wouldn't have drawn the entire building, only the part which would be recognizable. The symbol next to it looks like an old grave marker to me as well. If your great-grandfather drew this, it could indicate something with the lighthouse, or it may be a drawing of the old cemetery on lighthouse road. Of course, it wasn't abandoned and as creepy back then as it is now, but I believe it existed in 1910. Some of those grave markers may be original sandstone from the 1800's."

"That's an interesting thought," Megan said as she resolved to take a ride there the next day and see if there were any stones with her family's name on them. She knew where Rose and George were buried, and she was pretty sure the entire family was in the same large area at the St. Francis cemetery at the top of the hill. It was a gorgeous location with a permanent yet protected view of the ocean for all eternity.

"Who knows?" Doogie shrugged. "This can be anything from an original sketch of the area, before Misty Manor was built, to a specific treasure map, but I'll bet whatever it is, it may be worth something if you can find the rest of it. You should start going through some of the things in this house."

"I'm sure Megan will start as soon as she gets herself settled," Nick said as he changed the subject. "In the meantime, I've got a shift tomorrow morning, so I'll have to say goodnight soon."

Everyone got the hint and began to rise from the table. As the group ambled toward the front door, they continued to talk about how great the meal was and how much fun it was to get together as a group.

"I appreciate that you're listening to my ideas about getting rid of plastic on the beach, and I hope you'll consider being a champion to my cause," Doogie said.

"Absolutely," Megan said with a smile. "We'll get together again to form an action plan as soon as possible."

"I hope everyone here gets to be on the committee," Doogie said with a smile as he glanced at Georgie.

"As long as they want to, we'll need all the help we can get. Thanks again for the info about Misty Manor. I'll go to town hall tomorrow and see what I can find."

"Whatever you find, start making copies for your historical archives."

Marie met the group in the foyer hall and handed Tommy and Amber a large paper bag filled with containers of food. "Keep the bag upright, so nothing spills."

"You got it, Marie. We're going there right now," Tommy said as he grabbed the handles on the bag.

"Okay, hold the bottom and don't get it wet if you go by the beach."

Tommy looked at Amber and tilted his head toward the door. "We'd better go."

"Okay, I'm coming," Amber said as she hurried toward the door. She stopped to give Megan a quick hug. "It was a great night, thank you so much."

"Don't forget, I'll be dropping off those tickets next week," Tommy said as he grabbed Amber's hand and walked out the front door.

"Thank you again for a great night," Doogie said as he turned toward the door. He paused for an instant and looked at Georgie. "May I walk you home or to your car?"

"I'd like that," Georgie said as she offered a smile.

Megan and Nick watched as the two left the front porch, walked across the lawn to the beach and then onto the boardwalk toward Georgie's house.

Megan closed the front door. "Looks like that worked out better than you thought," Megan said as she elbowed Nick in the ribs.

"Time will tell."

"I thought you had to go to work in the morning."

"I do, but I was trying to get everyone moving. Good Lord, I thought we were going to be at that table forever."

Megan laughed. "I get it."

"Besides, I didn't want Doogie going too far when he was looking at the photo of the treasure map. I was surprised you showed it to him."

"It was only one little piece," Megan said as she shrugged her shoulders. "At least he explained the symbol, and as I said, I'll go to town hall tomorrow and see what I can find. While I'm there, I'll find out who owns the property for the cemetery as well."

"Okay, be safe," Nick said as he leaned down and rubbed noses with her before kissing her deeply. "I had a great night. We should do this more often except skip the company part. We could have dinner and move on from there."

"Yes, we could," Megan whispered. "But not tonight. It's been a long day, and you're working until the morning. Call me after work?"

"Within seconds," Nick said through a kiss while pressing her with his body.

A clang in the kitchen interrupted them. "Dudley, stop right there," Marie yelled as she chased the dog into the foyer. When she saw the couple, she abruptly stopped. "Oh, I'm sorry. I was trying to keep the pets in the kitchen."

Megan laughed as they separated, and Dudley jumped on her leg. "It's okay, Marie. He's been locked up all night. Dudley and I will walk Nick to his car."

Nick opened the front door, and the three piled out of the house. Dudley immediately barked and ran into the grass while Megan and Nick watched.

"He's probably flushing out birds," Megan said as she looked at the ocean.

"Most likely," Nick agreed as he shook his head. They held hands and enjoyed the breeze.

When Dudley returned from the weeds and a romp through the sand, Nick rubbed his head and turned to Megan. "Go ahead and get inside. I worry about you, so I'm going to wait here until you lock the door and set the alarm."

She stood on her toes for a kiss and turned to go as she whistled for Dudley. Nick stood, poised in the moonlight, scanning the beach as he watched them go. Once he heard the lock engaged, he turned and walked to his car.

CHAPTER 19

Sunshine woke Megan to the sound of crying seagulls and waves crashing to the shore. The breeze through the gauzy curtains was pleasant and refreshing. Rolling over, she was fixed with a laser stare from both Dudley and Smokey as they watched to see if she was getting out of bed for the day or a quick trip to the bathroom. When they realized she had rolled out of bed for good, they jumped up and followed her through her morning ritual and down the grand staircase in hopes of getting breakfast.

Megan walked to the back of the house and opened the door for Dudley who immediately ran out to a stand of trees. The magnificent smell of coffee reached her while she waited and she remembered Marie had stayed overnight after cleaning the dining room and kitchen. Megan opened the door and watched until Dudley returned to the porch.

Walking into the kitchen, she saw Marie at the stove once again. She was removing a small tray of cinnamon buns from the oven. "They smell marvelous," Megan said as she walked over to the coffee pot and grabbed a mug. She added coffee, cream, a small amount of sugar and sat at the kitchen table as Marie slid a plate with a warm pastry in front of her. "I shouldn't eat this, but it smells so good. Thank you."

"My pleasure," Marie said. "I'm sure you'll try to fast for a week now, so I thought I'd at least encourage a treat for breakfast."

"That you did," Megan said, talking with food in her mouth. Once she finished eating, she stood and gave Marie a big hug around the shoulders. "I can't tell you how delicious dinner was last night, and I appreciate all the effort you put into cooking for everyone."

"You had a good time?" Marie asked as she sipped her cup of coffee.

"Yes, it was a lot of fun," Megan said with a big smile.

"Be careful," Marie said dryly. "I've heard that smiling can be contagious. You don't want to pick that up as a habit."

Megan laughed. "Now, now, I've only tried it for one day."

"Seriously, it's nice to see you relax. We should make this a habit. You can entertain your friends at least once or twice a month, and I'll get to cook all sorts of yummy stuff."

"I'll see what I can do," Megan said as she placed her cup in the sink. "I have a few errands to run, so I hope you plan on doing something to relax. Go to the beach or take a nap. Don't worry about me."

"I won't," Marie said. "I'm going to dry the dishes and put everything away, and then I have a new book I want to start. My favorite rocking chair is waiting on the porch with a cold pitcher of lemonade, but I may have some guests coming to visit the beach. If so, I'll be home getting ready for them."

"Sounds great, please do have fun," Megan said as she scratched both pets on the head. "Would you mind keeping Dudley and Smokey company while you read?"

"Absolutely not," Marie said. "We'll have a good nap after lunch."

Megan laughed. "I'm sure you will." She gave Marie another hug before leaving the kitchen and heading for grandmother Rose's office off the foyer.

Megan sat at the desk and took in the little office, her office now. She hadn't been able to clean or organize the room since her grandmother's death, but after a year in mourning over losing her job, returning home, almost being killed, and her grandmother's death, Megan felt like she finally had a small window of hope standing before her. She wanted to document the history of her family, take over the foundation, restore the house and even build a relationship with Nick. Who knows what was around the corner, but she was finally ready to give life a try again.

Megan picked up the old-fashioned, heavy, black kettle phone on the desk and dialed Teddy. It was strange not using her cell phone, but she had left it upstairs and didn't want to waste time going back up to the third floor. Megan was pleased the phone still worked and vowed to keep it connected if the phone company continued to support the wiring.

After several rings, Teddy's voicemail picked up. Megan listened to his message, encouraging the caller to leave all information. Megan went into detail about questions regarding the history of her family, the deed to Misty Manor and wanting to champion Doogie's environmental cause of plastic on the beach. She explained she was going to town hall and the cemetery and asked Teddy to call her back as soon as he could.

CHAPTER 20

ircling the block one more time, Megan spotted someone pulling out of a metered parking spot. Parking was at a minimum in town during the summer due to the influx of tourists and summer residents. She had her blinker on and quickly pulled in when the other car left, despite someone leaning on their horn behind her. Although there was money on the meter, she added more for good measure and went into town hall.

The building was connected to the police department, and it was a court day. Dozens of people and their lawyers lined a room outside of court waiting to clear up business with the town judge. Megan kept moving to the other side of the building. She had never been there and had no idea where to go. She slowly walked by each office, tax assessor, records, permits, licensing, and suddenly found herself outside of the mayor's office. She cringed as she watched Andrew Davenport walk across his inner office and sit down at his desk. When he turned his head, she quickly dodged to the side of the door and walked away, her heart beating in her chest. He was the nastiest man she knew and had not been a friend of her family for years. The last person she wanted to run into would be him.

Megan made her way back to the records department and after a conversation with several people, was directed to someone who could help her find records pertaining to the original deed for Misty Manor and properties of Misty Point. She was informed they didn't have those documents in a filing cabinet, especially since they were a hundred years old, but the woman said she would speak to the administrator who could potentially allow her to search their stored digital information. Megan was also advised to go to the county office for information. Sighing, Megan had no choice but to leave her name and phone number and hope for the best. She resolved to call Teddy again as he must have some records of the house in his file.

Pulling out of the parking spot, she made her way through traffic in the center of town and down Main Street. She headed northeast around the bay toward higher land. Megan remembered the cemetery from when she grew up in Misty Point but was not one of the kids who would party there over the weekend and talk about it once they were back in school during the week. Beyond the fact that it was on Lighthouse Drive she had no specific knowledge whatsoever.

The bay was gorgeous, boasting an obvious high tide. Sailboats bobbed as families enjoyed the sun on the beach. Bay beach was a completely different experience than the beach in Misty Point. It was smaller and more of a place to read or hang out when someone wanted to get off their boat for a while. The marina had restaurants, bars, commercial vessels taking tourists for fishing and sightseeing tours as well as serving as home for those who lived on their boats for the summer months. New Jersey was too cold for someone to live on their boat year-round, so many owners left for warmer ports by September. Some of the Marina residents never graced the edge of the ocean during the summer. It wasn't Megan's favorite spot, but everyone had a different view of the shore they liked to worship each year.

Climbing the small elevation near the edge of town, Megan reached the turn to Lighthouse Drive. It was one of the only areas in town that was on a small cliff overlooking the north end of Misty Point as well as the gorgeous Atlantic Ocean. As a protected area, no one was able to build there, so it remained as nature intended it.

Megan pulled into the small parking lot which also served as a beautiful scenic view and a great place for photographers. There were some hiking trails in that area of town at the end of which was a bird sanctuary complete with a wooden boardwalk from which bird lovers could watch for favorite species all year long.

Megan parked the car, pulled out her cell phone and walked toward the cemetery. It was obvious the high school kids were still using the area as a meeting place each weekend. Trash lined the wild vegetation at the edge of the parking lot. There were no garbage cans in sight or any signs of care from the town. Megan reminded herself to ask Nick what he knew of the area.

Reaching the small cemetery, she pushed open the rusty gate which was practically leaning on its side. Years of neglect had allowed the post to sink into the ground. She made her way into the area and was glad she had worn long pants and sneakers. The sacred area had not had maintenance in years, so the wild grass was tall and flowing. There was no pattern to the gravestones that Megan could discern except for the small stone wall that outlined the area. Some head-stones were flat, some were crooked, and some were so old the wording was no longer legible.

Megan made her way to the far wall and was amazed to find a complete bird's eye view of Misty Manor, the lighthouse and her private property. Had the cemetery been clean and cultured, it would have been a beautiful place to spend eternity, but all her deceased relatives were located at St. Francis Cemetery.

Megan explored and looked for names on the headstones to see if any of them triggered a clue. Most only had dates. She realized the deceased must be a few generations old, but there was nothing which suggested the cemetery had anything to do with a treasure hunt or burial site.

Megan envisioned the book, *Treasure Island,* since that was the book which hid the lever in the bookcase. In case there was an easy clue, she looked for a headstone with a pirate name which might be a marker and not a personal headstone at all. She looked for Black-beard, Captain Flint, Long John Silver, Billy Bones, Jim Hawkins,

Robert Louis Stevenson and his friend, William Ernest Henley. She almost thought she had something when she found a grave marker with the initials J.H. but there was nothing distinctive about the head-stone that would lend a clue. She also didn't find anything labeled Hispaniola.

Laughing she asked herself what she expected to find. A big X on a gravestone or a parrot carved next to a name? What had she planned to do if she found one like that? She certainly wasn't prepared to start digging up graves to see if she found gold or Spanish coins.

Megan pulled out her cell phone and took a few photos of her property from the cliff and then of the cemetery itself in case she needed to recheck later. Once she was satisfied, she returned to her car and drove back to Misty Manor.

She walked up to the porch and opened the front door. Dudley and Smokey came running into the foyer and were very happy to see she had come home. She gave them both hugs and received dog kisses along with a healthy dose of drool from Dudley. Marie was nowhere to be found, but Megan saw a note on the refrigerator telling her that Marie had left for a while, but there were leftovers in the refrigerator for a sandwich or dinner. Opting for a low-calorie yogurt for herself, she gave the animals a snack and spent the next couple of hours in her grandmother's office, cleaning out drawers and filing papers. She was still hoping to find something significant to explain her questions.

The answering machine remained quiet as she worked, and she was a bit miffed she hadn't heard back from Teddy or the town hall. Checking her watch, she realized it was half past three, and she hadn't heard anything from Nick either. He had started work at 6:00 a.m. and should have finished by now. She lifted the receiver from the desk phone and immediately heard a dial tone. She also checked her cell phone and found full service was available. She simply wasn't being called.

While her cell phone was in her hand, she went to the photos app and looked at the photo she had taken of the treasure map. The photo only revealed the corner of the map, but once again she studied the symbols. They were varied, and she had no clue in what order they belong. There was a symbol which looked like a sun, another which looked like waves. She saw a ship, an eye, a tree, a rock, a bird and the lighthouse symbol. A trail connected all the symbols and ended at the lighthouse. Megan remembered being told the lighthouse on her property was built after Misty Manor, and she doubted any real pirate would have buried a treasure in an area which was active with builders and townspeople. There were no names or trademarks or branding she could find.

Sighing heavily, she closed the office and went onto the front porch with the pets to get a breath of fresh air. She sat in the rocking chair while Dudley and Smokey sprawled on the porch near her. Her cell phone began to ring, and she saw Nick's name pop up on the screen.

"Hello?" Megan asked as she placed her cell near her ear. Dudley's head popped up as he watched her sit forward.

"Hey, how are you?" Nick's voice drifted across the phone.

"I was waiting for you to call."

"That's why I'm calling, to tell you I can't talk," Nick said.

"That doesn't make sense. We are talking," Megan laughed.

"I know, but I can't stay on the phone," Nick whispered. "You'll hear about it soon enough, but I can only tell you we found a body today."

"That's terrible," Megan said, shock registering in her voice. "Thank goodness he wasn't at Misty Manor. I've had my share of dead bodies since I've come home. Was it an accident?"

"No, it looks like there was some violence involved."

"I don't believe it. Where did you find him?"

"Some kids found him this morning under the boardwalk."

"Aw, that's horrible. What's going on with this town?"

"Well, that's the only reason I'm calling. I wanted to warn you," Nick continued to whisper.

"Warn me? About what? That violence in Misty Point is escalating?"

"In case your buddy Mayor Davenport comes calling."

"Why would he come here? I know he wants to blame me for everything but believe me, this one has nothing to do with me."

"That's not entirely true."

"How can you say that?" Megan asked, her stomach knotting.

"The guy had nothing on him. No money, no identification, no drugs except a photo in his pocket."

"So?"

"The photo was of you, standing on the porch of Misty Manor."

Megan felt cold and was suddenly dizzy. She sat back in her rocker and closed her eyes.

"Megan, are you there? Say something."

Megan's mouth went dry, and her hands were shaking as she held the phone. "Nick, who is he and how does he have a photo of me?"

"We don't know yet, but we'll find out. I want you to go into the house, lock the door and don't answer to anyone until we sort this out. Someone said they thought he was a friend of Doogie's so I'm going to show him a photo and see if he can identify him. Maybe he had your photo because Doogie told him you would help with the plastic thing. I don't know. I don't want to assume it's a threat against you but go inside the house and put the alarm on until I get there."

Tears slid down Megan's face. Every time she felt she was finally moving on, something happened to slap her right back down. "Okay, Nick. I'll go inside and wait for you." She clicked off her phone, gathered her fur babies, headed into the house, locked the door and set the alarm. She then promptly ran to her room and sobbed.

CHAPTER 21

"Hey, can you get these people out of here?" Officer Peters turned around and pushed back the crowd while Captain Davis ducked underneath the boardwalk. He walked up to Nick who squatted in front of the victim. "Okay, what have we got here?"

"White male, thirty-five years old. Bunch of kids fooling around crawled under the boardwalk to beat buying a badge and ran into a dead body. Looks like he's been dead for a while. Rigor mortis has set in, so he's been dead at least four hours, but maybe longer from the looks of him. Plenty of lividity here," Nick said as he pointed to a part of the dead man's back.

The body was positioned on his side in a near fetal position. His hands were crossed over his abdomen. Dried blood covered the front of his body and was mixed with a significant amount of sand making a weird pasty substance. His eyes were open, and his death mask reflected one of surprise.

"Find any identification?" Davis asked as he pulled on a pair of black vinyl gloves to examine the body.

"We found nothing. No cash or cards so it could have been a robbery."

"How about a murder weapon?"

"We haven't found anything close to the body. It looks like he was stabbed but not sure with what. Probably bled out pretty quickly."

"Did he die here or was he dumped here?" Davis barked as he looked around. "I see a big pool of blood around the guy, and I don't see any drag marks."

"We didn't either, so whatever happened, it probably took place right here. The fact that he was under the boardwalk with someone to begin with, tells me he probably wasn't doing anything legal."

"Get out of my way, move it," a voice yelled from behind them.

"Uh-oh, looks like Chen is here," Nick said as he smirked.

Davis nodded and leaned back.

Chen arrived, saw Davis wearing gloves, and dropped a vinyl toolbox on the sand. "Are you screwing with my crime scene?"

Davis raised his hands to surrender. "Not me, I didn't touch the guy. I'm only looking at him."

"Yeah, but you're probably squatting in a prime part of the evidence field. Did you already take photos?"

"Yes, got thousands of them I think," Nick said. "We took as many as we could but don't forget a group of kids found him so who knows what they did before we got here. They thought he was drunk until someone went and checked him."

"I wanted to make sure the guy was dead," Davis said as he watched Chen pull a large thermometer out of his bag and stick it into the body, aiming for the liver.

"Chen, that's disgusting," Davis said as he shook his head.

"Once I get a body temp, I can make an educated guess as to how many hours he's been dead, but I'll have to get the conditions from last night. There was no rain here, right?"

"No, it was dry. The temperature stayed around 65 degrees overnight, with a slight breeze but we'll get an official report for you to work with," Nick said.

"Appreciate it," Chen said as he continued his preliminary screen. "Did you find anything else around him? Broken glass, liquor bottles, drug paraphernalia, cell phone?"

"Nothing," Nick said as he shook his head.

Chen checked the abdomen and then looked at the victim's back. "No exit wounds so most likely not shot, probably stabbed. Find his wallet?"

"No," Nick said as he pointed to a paper bag resting nearby.

"Anything in that bag?"

"Not much," Nick said with a shrug.

"What the hell does that mean? Was there something in there or not?"

"Not his wallet," Nick said retrieving the bag and handing it to Davis who still wore his gloves. "There's a photo inside."

"Here, use this," Chen said as he handed Davis a pair of tweezers. "Try not to touch it anywhere except in the very corner."

Davis tried to go into the bag with the tweezers, but his hand was shaking. "I feel like I'm playing that damn children's game about the surgeon trying to pull things out before the buzzer goes off."

Chen laughed. "We used to play that in medical school."

"Is that what you did in Yale?" Nick asked dryly.

"Amongst other fun things," Chen said while he watched Davis. "Maybe one day we'll have a drink, and I'll teach you a thing or two. Getting close Captain or what?"

Davis finally pulled out a rectangular piece of paper. As he held it up, Chen clicked on a flashlight and illuminated the paper. "Looks like a photo."

"Holy shit," Davis said. "I don't believe it. She's right in the middle of things again. Davenport is gonna go nuclear when he hears about this."

The three men continued to look at the photo which revealed an image of Misty Manor at dusk and standing on the porch was a clear shot of Megan Stanford with Dudley at her feet. A single drop of blood stained the corner of the photograph.

CHAPTER 22

*A*n hour later, Megan woke up with a headache. She had fallen asleep with her friends by her side. She slept but had not rested. Her nose was stuffy, and her eyes were puffy and swollen. She checked her phone, but there had not been any calls since Nick earlier in the afternoon. Groaning, she got up, went to the bathroom and headed toward the kitchen. Dudley and Smokey ran after her, hoping for a treat. She poured some dry food into each of their bowls but could barely concentrate as she was afraid of what Nick would eventually tell her.

Looking around, she realized Marie had never come back to Misty Manor. Megan picked up her phone and began to text.

Hey, did your guests arrive? If so, no need to come over, I'm here with the pets. Stay home and rest.

A few minutes later, she got a response.

Are you sure? I can bring dinner.

Megan answered.

Yes, we're good. We'll see you tomorrow.
Have a good night.

Megan sighed and barely put her phone down before it started ringing. Hoping it was Nick, she grabbed it and clicked the green button. "Nick?"

"Sorry to disappoint you," a loud voice boomed from the phone.

"Hello?" Megan asked as realization washed over her. "Ed?"

"You haven't forgotten me," Ed said, pleased that she remembered him.

Ed had been her immediate supervisor when she worked for the Detroit Virtual News. Trying to stay relevant and on top of a few juicy stories, their news manager had pushed them to dig up stories, to be truthful but be out there pounding the pavement, looking for news. Megan had stumbled on a story about a suspicious act by one of the newspaper owners, and she was promptly fired as a result. Despite the fact she had since inherited Misty Manor and two hundred million dollars, she was still peeved about being fired for doing her job. Ed had been the office bear, protecting his journalists, but this time he was no match for the owner. Losing the job was one thing, but Ed, who had always been like her overprotective uncle, had let her down. Megan realized it wasn't his fault she was fired, but she had been shocked and mortified when it happened.

"Of course, I haven't forgotten about you, Ed," Megan said softly.

"I hope you're not still mad at me. I did all I could to keep you with us, but I was loudly overruled."

"I figured that," Megan said. "Is this a pleasure call? How's Marge?"

"She's okay. She misses you terribly and wants you to come back."

"Well, I can honestly tell you that will never happen. Grandma Rose passed away, and I've inherited Misty Manor. I was raised in New Jersey, and now I'll stay in New Jersey."

"I'm very happy for you," Ed said. "I miss you, too, but I'm sure you're happy to be home."

"I am," Megan said, softly. "I am."

After a small pause, Ed broke the silence and said, "So this is awkward, but I hear that another dead body was found in Misty Point."

Surprised, Megan looked at the phone. "How the hell did you hear about that already? You have a net around me, Ed?"

He cleared his throat a couple of times before he answered. "It's possible we have an alert set for your name or Misty Point and such because we didn't want to lose contact, but I've got to say, your name has been popping up quite a bit lately."

Butterflies gripped Megan's stomach. "Why is that?"

"Well, news of a dead body travels fast. All we have is an alert some guy was found dead under the boardwalk. The other thing that's popped up on the web is that there's buried treasure in Misty Point."

Megan's face grew hot as she listened in disbelief. "That's ridiculous. We had a children's treasure hunt in town, but that was a recreational event for the kids."

"That's what I thought in the beginning, but this story is growing wings, and I thought I might as well ask you directly or warn you if that's the case. I don't know who started the story or why, but it's gone viral in the last twelve hours."

"I don't believe this," Megan said. "What does the story detail?"

Ed paused before he spoke. "The lead states there's a real treasure buried somewhere on Misty Point."

"Oh, my Lord," Megan said as her stomach clenched.

"Worse than that, someone's on the web trying to sell copies of a map for twenty-five dollars. The site screams scam from the minute you see it, but another story says there was an estate sale where someone found an old treasure map in a treasure chest and that there's an active treasure hunt going on. The story is fueling the gold rush type of thinking. Whoever finds it gets to keep the gold. The only reason I even considered the story is because there's a *NJtreasure* hashtag attached and now there's a dead body."

Megan remained quiet as he spoke, fuming over the rumors.

"So, is there any truth to that story or a tie into this dead body?" Ed asked gently. "I don't want you to think I'm calling to get a lead by the way. I've wanted to reach out to you for some time now, but if you want the truth out there, best to give it to a friend than another paper."

"What do you expect me to think? I've been here for a year, and it's the first time you've called. I've heard from Marge, but not from you, Ed. I don't know anything about treasure maps, gold or an estate sale, so you're barking up the wrong tree by calling me. If I hear anything, we can discuss it next time you call to check in."

"But you don't deny there's a dead body? Okay, don't get mad. Listen, I have a new cell phone. It's private. Let me give you the number. Write it down in case you ever need anything. Don't argue, just do it and keep it somewhere safe," Ed said as he rattled off the number.

Shaking her head, Megan wrote the number down although she was tempted to rip it up the moment she was done.

"I know your feelings were hurt, and things didn't end well, but I want us to be friends again. Keep my number, and if you want to talk, you can call me for any reason. Is that okay?"

"Yes, that's fine. I'll keep the number, but otherwise, I've got nothing to offer," Megan repeated.

"That's fine, I don't care about the story," Ed said. "I miss you, kid. Take care of yourself. I'll tell Marge you said, hello."

CHAPTER 23

*M*egan hung up the phone. She desperately needed to talk to Nick but didn't want to bother him if he was in the middle of an investigation. She picked up her phone to text him, but as she was pulling up his name, she heard a knock on the front door. Megan ran to the door and looked at the monitor which showed Nick outside. She quickly turned off the security system, opened the locks, dragged Nick into the house and threw her arms around him.

"I can't believe you're finally here," she said. "I've been on pins and needles all day. What happened?"

Nick leaned down and kissed her. "It's good to see you, too."

"I'm sorry, Nick," Megan said chagrined. "But I've been nervous ever since you called me, and I have more things to tell you."

Nick smiled as they walked into the kitchen. He pulled out a chair and sat down. Dudley immediately came over and placed his head on Nick's leg, hoping for a head scratch or even better for a treat. Megan opened the refrigerator door and looked inside.

"Iced tea? Or would you like a cold beer?"

"The beer sounds great, but who knows if Davis is going to call me, so I'd better have the iced tea."

She pulled a tall glass from the cabinet, added ice, lemon slices and filled it with the tea. "It's homemade and flavored with peach and raspberries, so I think you'll like it."

Nick picked up the glass and drank most of it in one long continuous pull. He placed the glass back on the table. "That was delicious and hit the spot. I didn't realize how thirsty I was, but it's pretty darn hot to be on the beach in a uniform all day."

Megan nodded and refilled the glass before pouring one for herself. She pulled out another chair and sat down at the table. After Nick had another long drink, he wiped his mouth with a napkin and looked up. "Okay, you go first. What else do you want to tell me?"

"I had a call today. A very unexpected and chilling phone call."

"From who?" Nick looked down as Smokey rubbed against his leg.

"My old boss, in Detroit. His name is Ed, and I may have mentioned him."

"I've heard his name before," Nick said, encouraging her to go on.

"He hasn't called in the year since I've been here, but he calls today to tell me he's sorry about what happened, and he hopes we can be friends again."

"And?"

"Yes, well that's the interesting part. Ed also managed to say, 'by the way, we've heard there's a treasure hunt going on in Misty Point, and now there's a dead body.'"

It was Nick's turn to look surprised. "Where was this man calling from?"

"Detroit. Can you believe it?"

"And how did he come by this information?"

"He's the manager of a newsroom. They have a ton of resources, but they also put a digital net around my name as well as the town and other keywords."

"What does that mean?"

"If anything pops up about me or any of the keywords on the internet, the newsroom will automatically get notified. Anyway, he said there was a story about a treasure hunt in Misty Point, and then the story about the dead body popped up as well. Thank you, social media."

"I get it," Nick said nodding his head.

"What's going on? I told Ed I didn't know anything about a dead body, but you had called earlier, so I knew something had happened. I can't tell you how upset I am that a photo of Misty Manor and me was in his possession. So, what happened?"

"As you know, we did find a body. Don't tell anyone I told you this and I mean anyone because I could get in trouble, but it looks like the guy was stabbed."

"Oh no, but why?"

"Hopefully we'll figure that out when we solve the case," Nick said. "But what is this about a treasure hunt?"

"I don't know, and I hope the two aren't related," Megan said as she collected the glasses and put them in the sink. "I tried to tell Ed we recently had a treasure hunt for kids run by the recreation department. He didn't buy it. According to him, there's gold to be found in Misty Point."

"Come to think of it, the town did seem busier than usual today," Nick said. "I hope they aren't coming into town thinking there's a real treasure."

Megan stood at the sink and rinsed the dishes. She appeared deep in thought as she dried the glasses and sat down at the table.

"What's on your mind?"

"It's obvious this rumor is the result of our search of the secret room off the library and the treasure map," Megan said as she held her head in her hands.

"We don't even know if there's a real treasure," Nick said. "How could it be that map?"

"If it was, someone had to squeal," Megan pointed out. "But who?"

"Could be anyone," Nick said. "There were four of us the first time we went in. Then you showed the little map to Doogie. Does Marie or your friends know anything about the map we found?"

"No, no one knows anything," Megan said. "I haven't told anyone, and Nathan signed the agreement which Jonathan brought with him."

"That leaves Jonathan himself. I don't trust the guy as far as I can throw him, and I don't know Doogie that well either. Who knows if he was mouthing off?"

"Nick, it doesn't have to be like that. We both know if someone tells someone else a fact the third person can grossly distort it. Then the rumor or story takes on a life of its own."

"It's a problem if the rumor is strong enough that someone is murdered as a result."

"That makes me feel terrible," Megan said. "Were you able to get anywhere in the investigation today?"

"No, Chen came to the crime scene. It was a hard scene to process because of the sand, the wind and all the people standing around taking photos with their cell phones. They were probably live streaming the event. Thankfully, it's dark under the boardwalk when you try to look in from five hundred feet away."

"Oh boy," Megan said as she cupped her chin with her hand.

"Then, your buddy showed up," Nick said with a smirk.

"Which buddy is that?"

"Mayor Davenport, of course. He wanted to see what all the excitement was about, and he'll never miss a photo op. He was right in the mix when they removed the body." Nick looked at his watch. "We should probably put the news on to see what they're reporting."

"Okay, let's go." Megan stood up, and the two of them walked into the living room where a flat screen television was mounted on a wall over the fireplace. She picked up the remote and flipped through several channels until she found the news. The reporter started the headlines and finally mentioned a murder at the shore.

"I'm sure they're saving the story for the end of the broadcast, so they don't lose viewers. We could search the web if you want to see what's been posted," Megan suggested.

"No, unless they have some cold hard facts, I'm not interested in everyone's opinion about everything that's happened since the birth of mankind." Nick looked at his watch. "I've got to get my stuff and change. Have you had any dinner?"

"No, I haven't. I was so upset I didn't eat, and I haven't given the pets a good meal."

"Why don't you get their food ready? I'll take Dudley outside with me, and we'll be back in a few minutes."

"You're changing here?" Megan asked.

Nick stopped and turned around. "Oh, didn't I tell you? I'm not only changing here, I'm moving in for right now. With all the crazy stuff going on in this town, there's no way in hell I'm leaving you alone in a big place like this."

CHAPTER 24

*M*egan placed the pizza box on the table while Nick poured the wine. They had ordered the food when Nick walked back into Misty Manor with a duffel bag packed with clothes and the things he needed to stay for a couple of days. They decided to eat in the solarium with the lights turned low. They sat by the floor to ceiling windows and slid open the French door to feel the breeze and listen to the soothing sound of the waves. Dudley and Smokey sat nearby. As Megan placed a slice of pizza on each plate, Nick picked up the glasses of wine and handed one over. "Cheers."

"I wish," Megan said as she took a sip of her wine. She picked up a plate and handed it to Nick. She then took the other plate, and the two sat on the couch to watch the beach in semi-darkness. Normally they wouldn't be able to see much, but the moon was full, and the light rotating from the lighthouse did a nice job of illuminating the beach and water.

They sat in silence for a while as they enjoyed their pizza and wine with the sound of the ocean. The combination relaxed Megan and made her feel sleepy. While they ate, Dudley stood up and whined as he looked out the window. He suddenly offered a sharp bark. Nick put down his plate and glass and told Megan to move away from the window. As she stood, she stiffened when she caught a glimpse of two people on the beach near the house. They appeared to be arguing, but she wasn't sure. Nick pushed her away from the window and back to the brick fireplace wall.

"Stay away from the window." He quickly ran out of the room, and Megan realized he was still wearing his shoulder holster and gun. She heard Nick run down the foyer and out the back door of Misty Manor. After five minutes or so, she heard loud noises and then people walking up the front steps. She wanted to look out the window, but Nick didn't want her near the glass so that she couldn't be a target. Within a few seconds, she heard the front doorknob turning, and she started to shake. The door burst open, and Nick walked through with a couple of women.

"Hey, big guy, hands-off," said a female followed by giggling. Megan inched toward the foyer and looked around the corner to find Nick by the door with Georgie and Amber. Letting out a large sigh and dropping her shoulders, she walked over to the trio.

"Look who I found lurking around the house," Nick said as he nodded toward her friends.

"We weren't lurking," Georgie said with a laugh. "We were on our way over to see what you were up to."

"That's the truth," Amber agreed as they followed Megan into the solarium.

"Well, they looked suspicious to me," Nick said with a wicked smile behind their backs.

Amber looked around the room and said, "Nick's mad because we broke up their little party.

"No, he's not," Megan said. "He's worried about me. There's a lot of weird stuff going on."

"Isn't there always around you?" Amber asked as she rolled her eyes toward Georgie who burst out laughing.

"She may have a point there." Georgie adopted a sympathetic look as she shrugged her shoulders.

"Oh, clam up," Megan said. "You guys want something to eat or drink?"

"I'll take a glass of wine," Amber said looking at the pizza box.

"And she'll smell one of your finest slices of pizza," Georgie said. "That way, they'll be no calories. I, on the other hand, will have pizza and wine if there's enough."

Shaking her head, Megan opened another bottle of wine and poured a glass for each one of her friends. She handed Georgie a full slice and cut a piece for Amber that was the size of a credit card.

"Have a seat, ladies," Megan said. "What's up?"

"We wanted to see how you were," Georgie said. "We didn't hear from you all day, which is a bit odd."

"Oh, I was busy, but now that you're here, I wanted to know how your night was after you left here with Doogie," Megan teased as she stared at her friend. "Before you start, let me say how nice it was to see you wearing regular makeup and not thick white cream over your nose."

Georgie smirked. "You know I have to wear sunblock on the beach. Besides, it's part of the lifeguard uniform."

"Yes, I could imagine you and Doogie sitting out there with matching noses," Megan said while Amber laughed at the visual. "So, what did you do last night?"

"As a matter of fact, I'm interested in that myself," Nick said as he tilted his head.

Georgie looked at Nick and shook her head. "Oh, no. I'm not saying anything with that look on your face. Maybe you should tell us what's going on. There's an awful lot of rumors going on around town." Georgie took another bite of pizza and waited.

Megan looked at Nick and said, "We may as well tell them. They're going to hear gossip anyway."

"Oh my, you two eloped?" Amber's mouth remained slightly open in anticipation of the news.

"Who? Me and Megan? Not yet, but maybe next week," Nick said as he swiped another piece of pizza out of the box.

"Really?" Georgie asked, eyes wide.

"No, not really." Megan put her hand on her hips. "Sit down so I can explain what's going on, but you can't tell anyone." Megan poured another glass of wine for everyone as they sat, and she began to explain everything from the beginning. She started with Nathan's first visit to the library to finding the secret room and their first videotaped search. She recounted the safe and finding the small treasure chest with the jade turtle sitting on top of the treasure map.

"Is that what you were showing Doogie a photo of last night?" Georgie asked as she crossed her arms.

"Yes, but I only showed him a piece of it. I wanted to see if he thought it was authentic."

"Apparently he did because he talked about it on our entire walk back to my place," Georgie said.

"Oh? Then what happened?" Amber asked with a smirk.

"Yes, what did happen?" Nick asked. "How long did he stay with you?"

"Excuse me?" Georgie asked Nick as she looked at him.

Nick shrugged. "Just asking, that's all."

"Not that it's any of your business, but he didn't stay too long. It wasn't like it was an official date or anything. We chatted a bit, he asked for my number, and then he left."

"Do you know what time that was?" Nick asked.

Georgie frowned. "I don't know, ten o'clock? Why are you asking me this? I expect it from them, but from you, there's a whole different slant here."

"I can't stand it anymore," Megan said. "Georgie, weren't you at the beach today? Didn't you hear anything about a dead body under the boardwalk?"

"I wasn't on the beach today, but I did hear about the dead body, and then I heard about a treasure map which sounded similar to what Doogie was talking about on the way home and oh, I get where you're coming from now."

"Who was the dead guy?" Amber asked. "Do we know him?"

Nick shook his head. "I didn't know him, and he didn't have any identification on him. There were no money or credit cards, so I don't know if it was a robbery gone bad or something else. Someone thought he might be a surfer, and Doogie knew him, but we couldn't find Doogie anywhere, and he didn't answer his phone."

Georgie cleared her throat and looked down at her feet. "Oh, I can fill you in on that."

"I thought you said he went home at 10:00 p.m.," Amber said with her mouth open with a shocked face.

"He did, so stop and clear your dirty little mind. He called me this morning and asked if I wanted to take a ride with him today."

"Mind telling me where you went?" Nick said as he watched Georgie.

Georgie put her wine glass down and looked at Nick. "This is making me feel very uncomfortable. If you want to talk as a friend, I'll tell you whatever you want to know, but stop grilling me like I'm down in the station."

The room was quiet for a moment with an awkward pause before Nick put his hands up to surrender. "Fine, I want to know what Doogie was up to today. The police were called about a body. At first, someone thought Doogie might be able to identify him, but then Doogie's name came up repeatedly, so now Davis wants a sit down with him. And to be honest, I was taking advantage of your story to see if it'll match what he has to say. So, where did you go today?"

Georgie took a deep breath. "My story? You're insulting, but what the hell, I don't have anything to hide. We took a ride up to the Delaware Water Gap. We hiked a couple of trails and then rented a canoe and paddled the river a bit. We stopped at a little place for a great burger and then drove back down to the shore but wound up sitting in a ton of traffic on the Garden State Parkway. Are you happy now?"

"That's true, because Georgie and I had planned on coming over to Misty Manor earlier, but she was late which is why we were sniping on the way over," Amber said.

"Thank you," Nick said. "I appreciate it."

Georgie bristled. "Well, next time ask me nicely. I've got nothing to hide, and I just met the guy, so I'm not going to lie for him."

Nick pulled Georgie into a hug. "I'm sorry. I won't play tough cop around you anymore."

"Good, can we move on? What's going on? I'm confused between the dead body and the treasure and whatever the hell else is happening."

Megan jumped in to continue the explanation. "The point is we found this treasure map and started wondering if it could be real. That's one of the reasons I wanted to hear Doogie's talk about shipwrecks in the area. I also wanted to see if he could make any heads or tails of the symbols on the map."

"It sounds like you should pull it out and see if you can figure the damn thing out," Georgie said.

"That's what we're trying to do. I went to town hall today, as Doogie suggested when I asked about the history of the house and town, but then I almost ran into Mayor Davenport, so I scurried out of there." Megan rolled her eyes. "I'm interested in my family's history, but now it's a circus about the treasure."

"I think we have to talk to Teddy about all this," Nick said. "Before we pull out the map or do anything else. Let's be sure we meet with him tomorrow and get some questions answered."

"I agree, we'll call him first thing in the morning," Megan said. "Jonathan must have shown him the video by now and asked him about historical documents. He should have called me, but he didn't, so we'll call him tomorrow."

"Maybe he's out of town," Amber suggested. "A lot of people are on vacation."

"If so, Jonathan should have called to let me know."

"Let's let it go for tonight," Nick said as emptied the wine bottles between the glasses on the table.

"That from the man who's grilling me," Georgie said as she picked up the glass.

"Let's go outside for some fresh air," Amber said as she opened the French doors and walked out on the porch. She walked to one of the rocking chairs and sat down with her wine glass. "It's so beautiful out here, tonight."

The rest of the group followed and stood by the rail or sat in a rocker. Megan brought Dudley outside with her and let the dog go romping on the beach and sniff the weeds.

"When the moon is out, and the weather is calm, you have a perfect house on a perfect part of beach here," Georgie said dreamily. "I don't think I could ever move away from the beach, it's been in my blood for so long."

"Why? Are you thinking of moving?" Megan asked while she sipped her wine.

Georgie looked up and smiled. "No, but my mother keeps asking when I'm going to grow up and get a real job. Then I met Doogie, and you never know, maybe there's hope for me yet. But even if we kept seeing each other, I wonder what we'd do or where we'd live if we ever got married."

"With Doogie, you'd never leave the beach," Amber said. "The two of you would be here on orthopedic surfboards in forty years. That's a great idea. Start developing something for elderly surfers like you. Maybe, you'll get rich." Amber chuckled at her idea.

"Oh, shut up," Georgie said as she drained her glass. "I think it's time to call it a night."

"Yeah, I agree," Amber said. "I have to be at the office early tomorrow morning. It's my turn to bring snacks for the morning huddle, and then I'm on kitchen duty for the week."

"Sounds interesting," Megan said, rolling her eyes as she collected wine glasses.

"It sucks," Amber said. "I have beautiful clothes, but I'm not going to wear any of my designer things this week. With my luck, I'd spill milk while I'm trying to set up the coffee."

Nick chuckled. "I'll bet it's a lot better than the sludge they have at the station."

Amber paused for a moment before she nodded. "You're probably right about that."

Georgie pulled on Amber's arm. "C'mon, let's go."

"Okay, give me a minute to put my shoes on," Amber said as she slipped into expensive sandals. She turned and hugged Megan and lightly punched Nick on the arm. "Have a good night you two. Let us know what you find out tomorrow from Teddy, but in the meantime, mum's the word."

"Yes, mum's the word," Megan said as she watched her two friends descend the steps and walk across the beach. She wasn't sure, but the words brought back by the wind sounded as if they were sniping at each other again.

"Lot of emotion, tonight," Megan said as she turned back toward Nick. "Must be the moon."

"I don't know what it is, but summers at the beach are insane," Nick said as he collected the glasses. He turned to go inside, and Megan and Dudley followed him. Smokey was lying on the floor, in the solarium, near the French doors, watching the activities and enjoying the breeze. They walked to the kitchen and threw the dirty glasses and utensils in the sink. Megan set about washing dishes while Nick picked up the water bowls for the animals so Megan could refill them with cool, fresh water.

When they were finished, they turned out the kitchen lights, walked across the foyer and started up the grand staircase. "My, aren't we the domesticated couple?" Megan asked as they turned out lights as they went.

"It's not such a horrible idea," Nick said as he shifted his overnight bag on his shoulder. "You never know."

Megan felt a flush from her toes to her face.

"No comment?" Nick looked over at her as they continued to climb.

"I'm waiting for my heart rate to slow down," Megan said with a nervous chuckle.

"I'm surprised you're not lonely," Nick said. "The house is gorgeous, but you've got four floors counting the attic and about twenty-five rooms. Don't you ever get nervous staying here by yourself? It's awfully quiet."

They reached the third floor and headed toward the bedroom. They hadn't talked about Nick staying there or any specific plans for the evening. Megan was more nervous tonight than she had ever been in the past, but she didn't want Nick to know that. She stopped and turned to face him. "Honestly, I was so messed up when I came back to New Jersey and everything that's happened since, I haven't had time to settle down and notice everything going on around me."

Nick smiled and nodded for her to move forward. Face still flushed, she took a deep breath and then stopped again when Nick turned into the bedroom next to hers. He looked up and said to her, "I'm sleeping in here tonight. I know I stayed in a room on the second floor the last time I was here, but with all the crazy stuff going on, I'm staying near you."

"I'm not sure the linens are clean," Megan stammered.

"It's okay, if you get a fresh set of sheets for me, I'll change them before I go to bed." Nick was amused at her nervousness. "Unless you want me to sleep in your room?"

"Let me check the closet," Megan said as she scurried out of the room. Nick laughed and tossed his overnight bag onto a chair and stretched. It had been a long day, and he was tired. Megan returned to the room with a fresh set of linens and towels. Together they turned down the duvet and remade the bed. "No one's slept in this room for a long time although I'm sure Marie cleaned it a short while ago."

"Speaking of cleaning up, I'd like to take a shower. It was a long day with that dead body."

"Of course, you know where the bathroom is," Megan said as she pointed down the hall. "Give me ten minutes to go in there and clean it up. Speaking of dead bodies, did you hear anything else from Davis or the station?"

"No, not yet. Maybe they'll have some info at morning report." Nick unzipped his bag and pulled out shorts and a t-shirt. Megan watched, eyes wide. When he turned around, she blushed.

"Oh, let me get to the bathroom." Megan fled the room and Nick could hear her picking things up and the lid of the hamper closing. He thought he also heard the creak of the medicine cabinet mirror door. Several minutes later, he heard her shout, "All clear."

When Nick went into the bathroom and closed the door, she flew into her bedroom. She quickly straightened up and tried to decide what to do. She finally changed into day pajamas and sat on the bed as she waited for Nick, although she didn't know what to expect. A few minutes later, she turned her light off, leaned back against the pillows and relaxed. Dudley and Smokey immediately jumped on the bed to settle in for the night. With the small light from the bedside lamp, she nervously waited for Nick to finish in the bathroom. She sat up when she heard the door open. Wearing a fresh t-shirt and shorts, he stopped at the door of her room where she got up to meet him. His hair and skin were warm and damp, and he smelled great. He put his arms around her, and she leaned her head against his chest. After a minute of silence, he pushed back a few inches and leaned down. His lips found hers in a perfect kiss. When they pulled apart, he smiled, waited a few seconds, then kissed her on the nose and said, "goodnight."

Her heart beating wildly, she frowned and said, "What?"

"I'm hitting the hay. I've got roll call at 6:00 a.m. and you've got several animals on your bed waiting for you to join them." He then chuckled, kissed her cheek and left her room.

CHAPTER 25

The next morning, Megan felt a warm body lying against her back, and she snapped awake. She rolled over to see Dudley lying directly against her. The bedside clock said 7:30 a.m. and she quickly rolled out of bed. The pets raised their heads to see what the commotion was all about. Megan had to make a quick trip to the bathroom where she saw a wet toothbrush and the folded towels resting against the tub.

After using the facilities, she walked back toward her room, deliberately passing the doorway and stopping at the room next door. She shyly looked around the doorway and realized the room was empty. The bed was made. She felt a small pang of disappointment but then cheered up when she spied Nick's bag on a chair in the corner. She remembered he had roll call early this morning but her excitement at knowing he was coming back surprised her more than she expected.

She turned when she heard small footsteps in the hall and found a confused dog and cat staring at her. "Okay, you guys. Let's go downstairs and start the day."

CHAPTER 26

"About time you showed up," Davis said as he looked over at Nick standing in the doorway. Davis took a bite out of a large donut and chugged coffee from a paper cup.

Nick looked at his watch. "I'm only five minutes late, boss."

"Hmm, where the hell were you last night?"

"What do you mean?"

"I stopped at your house late last night, but no one was home." Davis took another bite of his frosted chocolate donut as he watched Nick's face.

Realizing he was turning red, Nick said, "I went to see Megan."

"Oh, nice," Davis said fixing Nick with a grin that made him turn and walk away.

When Davis finished his donut, he stood up and began to call for everyone's attention for morning report. Before he could get started, the door to the room banged open and in strode Mayor Andrew Davenport, looking very aggravated.

"Mayor? What can I do for you?" Davis asked as he turned to face him.

"You can solve another damn murder, that's what you can do." Davenport turned to face Nick who had walked up to the front of the room to claim his seat. "Might I point out, the third murder since your friend came back to town."

"So, what does she have to do with it?" Nick's nostrils flared as he adopted a defensive posture.

"That's what I want to know. I wanted to join morning report so that I could hear the latest details for myself." Davenport sat down on one of the tables and crossed his arms as he looked at Davis. "Please, don't let me interrupt you. Carry on."

"Suit yourself." Davis scowled, then turned and went to the podium at the front of the room. He cleared his throat to get everyone's attention. "Listen up, we've got a busy day out there." Davis went through roll call and made sure every officer had shown up for work. He reviewed the assignments for the day before he began to talk about specific crimes. "As you know, we caught a body under the boardwalk yesterday. We were able to get an identification using his fingerprints. Our John Doe is none other than Wade Wilton, an ex-con who was recently released for breaking and entering, robbery and theft. He had no wallet, money or credit cards, so we don't know if he was rolled or didn't have anything to carry. The only thing in his possession was a photo of Misty Manor." At this statement, he offered Nick a pointed look. "We do not have a murder weapon. The medical examiner will do the post, and we'll be looking for acquaintances and family. We believe this to be an isolated incident. Keep an ear out for chatter. You never know, we may catch a break."

Davis covered a variety of other crimes and problems that had been occurring around town and then dismissed the group to get to work. Once they all dispersed, he walked over to Nick and guided him into his office. "I want you to go to the jail today. Talk to this guy's parole officer. Find out who he was hanging out with and who shared his cell. There's an obvious connection here, and we're going to find out what it is."

"Gentlemen, may I have a moment?"

Nick and Davis turned around to find the mayor standing in the doorway. "Andrew, how can we help you?"

Davenport scowled and walked up to the desk. "I want to know what the hell is going on." He turned toward Nick. "Another body, more negative press and I'm sick of your girlfriend being in the middle of it. She's making a joke out of this town. Did you see the video out there? Now they're saying we have real gold hidden around town, so every low life and drifter is going to head our way." He jabbed the desk with his index finger as he got closer to Nick's face. "I don't know what kind of game she's playing, but I want it to stop now."

Nick clenched his jaw but kept his mouth shut as his eyes flicked toward Davis who gave him a warning look. Davis came around the desk and put an arm around the mayor to guide him toward the door. "Andrew, we'll look into this situation immediately, but I'm sure you have more important things to do than worry about our investigation. You'll be the first person we'll call when we have some answers. Trust me." He walked Davenport into the hallway and directed him toward his office. Davis then came back to find Nick fuming.

"That low life son of a..."

"Nick, he's an ass. I wouldn't give the guy the time of day. He doesn't give a hoot about the dead guy except that it makes his record look bad, but I do have to say, Megan certainly has a knack for being connected to dead bodies."

"That's not her fault. For cryin' out loud, she owns over half the town, so if you use that criterion, she's going to be connected to almost anything that happens in Misty Point. Her family built the town, and she helps to support it through her grandmother's charities."

"You got a point there," Davis said.

"The reason I was there last night is she's in that large house by herself with a couple of near break-ins and wise guys hanging around. I'm concerned for her safety, and that ass is only concerned about his reputation."

"That's interesting," Davis said. "What kind of break-ins? You think Wilton was part of that?"

Nick shook his head. "I don't know. She was catching some crap the other day from a guy she hired to help her start renovating Misty Manor. I happened to be there, so I threw the guy out."

"Does this guy have a name?"

"Graham, Nathan Graham," Nick said with a toss of his head.

Davis was quiet for a moment. "I think I know the guy. I'll send Peters over to talk to him." Davis walked around his desk and sat down. "What about this Doogie Portman? Is he a problem?"

"I don't think so. He grew up here and then became a professional surfer. He's been on the surfing circuit but recently retired and has come back to Misty Point. He was invited to Misty a couple of nights ago. Megan had Marie make a little dinner for a few of us."

"What's all this bull about gold and a treasure?"

Nick groaned and rolled his eyes. "When Nathan was there one day, we found some of her great-grandfather's possessions in a room off the library. One of the papers could have been a little treasure map, but no one could make heads or tails of it. Then, Megan went to see Doogie's talk on Sunday about shipwrecks around the turn of the century. She invited a group of us to dinner, and she showed him a part of the map. We don't even know if it's real. The next day, a story is on social media about gold treasure and the dead guy is found under the boardwalk."

"Who else was at this dinner?" Davis asked grabbing a pencil and a pad.

Nick sighed. "Megan, Amber, Georgie, Tommy, Doogie and me."

"Did anyone else know about this before the social media?"

"Nathan Graham and Jonathan Brandon Carter were there originally. Marie O'Sullivan was in the kitchen. I don't think she heard anything, but you never know."

"She doesn't strike me as the social media type," Davis said as he wrote the names on his pad. "All it takes is for one person to say something that gets blown up each time the story is repeated, and you have a full-blown crisis on your hands." Davis threw the pencil on his desk and looked up at Nick. "As I said, I want you to reach out to the jail and Wilton's parole officer. Let's connect the dots. Hopefully, we can dispel this rumor and concentrate on finding a killer instead."

"You got it, Captain," Nick said as he stood and headed out the door.

"Nick," Davis yelled out.

Nick stopped and turned around to face Davis. "Yeah?"

"You better not be holding anything back on this story."

Nick scowled again and without speaking turned back toward his desk, picked up his keys and headed out of the station.

CHAPTER 27

$\mathcal{M}$egan put up a pot of coffee as she tried to plan her day. What started as an interesting discovery in her family home had already morphed into a ridiculous situation between the treasure hunt and a dead body. Megan was afraid to consider a murder had occurred in town based upon the same discovery and distorted rumors that grew as a result.

She fed both pets and then escorted Dudley to the door so that he could relieve himself. When he raced back inside, they returned to the kitchen, and she poured a large cup of coffee. She moved to the porch, sat in one of the rockers and enjoyed her morning brew while trying to figure out what to do next.

She spent fifteen minutes watching the seagulls circle the beach looking for food as the waves crashed to shore. She watched the waves roll in and saw many boats as they left the protective channel to sail into ocean waters for the day. She realized she felt relaxed, and despite being unsettled, she felt like she was home. Her home, her destiny, her future.

Finishing the coffee, she went inside, did the dishes and went to her grandmother's office. She sat at the desk and looked around the office again. She imagined how it would look if she remodeled it the way she wanted. It would be decorated to make her feel excited to work there on a regular basis. It was time to let go of her guilt for moving on and living her life.

Megan picked up the phone and placed a call to Teddy. Surprised that he answered, she arranged for him to come to Misty Manor to discuss the estate's affairs later that morning. She explained she was looking for historical information for the estate and any he had for the family. They hung up, and Megan realized she wasn't sure if Jonathan would be coming as well, but it didn't matter. She needed to know what was going on with the estate. It was her responsibility now. She hadn't spent a dime, and she felt guilty to think about it, but times had changed.

When she realized she was hungry, she went into the kitchen to grab a snack. In the refrigerator, she found more food packaged and dated to be delivered to Billy. Now she realized how Billy was getting decent meals. She smacked herself in the head for not thinking of asking Marie earlier. Megan stopped what she was doing and decided to deliver the food to Billy immediately.

She pulled large bags with handles from the closet and began to pack the leftover food. Adding whatever she thought would bring comfort or enjoyment to Billy, she brought the bags to the front door. She then flew upstairs and made sure she was dressed for the day. She would visit with Billy and then return to see Teddy. She was hoping to gain some serious information from both men about her family and the murder.

CHAPTER 28

*N*ick arrived at the county jail and parked his car. After showing proper identification, he was allowed past a tall fence topped with razor wire and led toward a shabby building with bars across windows layered with grime and dirt.

He chose not to sit in one of the molded plastic chairs assuming they hadn't been wiped down or cleaned since they were originally placed in the room.

After a few moments, a door to one of the offices sheltered by a long, scarred wooden counter opened and a man looked out. He beckoned the security guard to escort Nick past the counter and into the office.

The two men briefly shook hands while sizing each other up. Nick wearing his uniform, the man dressed in street clothes. "Nick Taylor, Misty Point Police Department," Nick said as he introduced himself. "Thanks for taking the time to meet with me."

"No problem," the man said as he indicated a chair for Nick to have a seat. "Manuel Rodrigues but you call me Manny. What can I do for you?"

"I'm trying to get some information on a body found under our boardwalk. Wade Wilton. He was recently paroled?"

Manny nodded his head. "That's correct, he was here a couple of months. Not a model prisoner but we've had worse." Manny pulled a set of papers from the side of his desk and tossed it toward Nick. "When I got your request, I asked for his file. He's had some scrapes in here, and you'll find the names of the people he hung out with. What happened to him?"

"I'm not sure yet," Nick said as he watched Manny. "The post hasn't been completed, but it looks like he was stabbed. I'm looking to see if there's any specific connection to Misty Point, NJ. Any reason he'd be hanging around there or looking for trouble?"

"As I said, I didn't see anything obvious, but you may pick up something different. I didn't see any family listed either. I'm not sure if he doesn't have any or if they cut him off. Did you guys do a notification?" Manny watched Nick as he shifted through the paperwork. "That's not the full file, just some notes from his parole officer. The full file probably won't get here for another couple of days. You'd have to come back if you want to look through that."

Nick nodded his understanding as he quickly scanned the few papers in front of him. The victim was raised in New Jersey and was not a stranger to jail. Multiple charges of breaking and entering with intent to commit a felony. He'd been in and out of the system numerous times. He was thirty-eight years old, and his home address listed him as homeless. A social worker had steered him toward several community programs which would provide residence in a temporary shelter until he managed to connect to a monitored job and find something slightly less meager for existence. Nothing in the file led Nick to believe Wilton had any specific reason to be in Misty Point beyond the typical reason anyone visits the shore on a regular basis.

"Did you know this guy?" Nick looked at Manny.

Manny shook his head. "No, he wasn't on my roster, but I didn't hear any major complaints about him in our briefings. It doesn't look like drugs were an issue, but he's no stranger to the system."

"When did he get out?"

"About a month ago. He had regular visits set up with his parole officer, James Smith. You need to come back in a couple of days and see what he has on permanent file. Make sure you ask for Smitty. He knows his parolees well."

Nick nodded and handed back the sheaf of papers. "I'll do that. There has to be a connection somewhere." Nick gave Manny his number and then shook his hand. "I appreciate you meeting with me. I'll be back to meet with Smitty when he gets here."

"I'll call you," Manny said as he memorized the number.

Nick nodded and walked toward the exit.

CHAPTER 29

*A*fter dressing for the day, Megan ran down to the foyer. The large shopping bags were waiting where she left them, but she gave them one last glance. Each item was packed carefully in aluminum foil, so Billy had little to do when he was ready to eat. Megan had no idea what Billy had in the lighthouse in the way of kitchen utensils. She also didn't know if Billy was on any medication or had to avoid certain foods or alcohol, but she planned to ask.

Calling Dudley, she picked up the bags and opened the door. The sunshine was bright, the breeze warm and the waves continued to curl on the shore. Dudley followed as she stepped onto the porch and locked the door behind her. As they walked over the grass and toward the sand, the seagulls began to swoop around them hoping for a tasty treat from the bag.

Dudley jumped up on occasion as the gulls passed overhead. He considered them his friends and loved the freedom of running and chasing them on the beach. The poor dog deserved nothing less after being kept in a cage for far too long, and Megan smiled as she watched him play.

They made their way to the lighthouse and up the stairs to the front door. Billy lived there most of his life in loyal servitude to the

Stanford family but would not have it any other way. He considered the position of lighthouse keeper the job of his dreams. One he loved to perform, get paid for and use as a permanent home. Now that he was in his eighties, he didn't want to give up his lighthouse home. Thankfully, the building stood on Stanford land and his nephew Tommy worked with him regularly to keep the lighthouse running in proper order.

At some point, Billy had a uniform as lighthouse keeper with a proper dark blue, kersey double-breasted coat, vest, trousers, and cap. He wore other clothes when he was working with oil and cleaning the lens. But years had gone by, and lighthouses had become automated. Billy refused to leave Misty Manor and the sea. Much like Grandmother Rose.

Megan used her set of keys to open the front door. She went inside with Dudley and called out to Billy as she started climbing the circular steps toward his apartment. Dudley had been there once before and whined for a moment before starting to climb the metal steps. As they ascended, Megan took notice of the brick interior as well as the beautifully carved arches surrounding the windows. There were archways in the base of the lighthouse as well as small, round carved openings on the floor.

Reaching the apartment, Megan knocked and called Billy's name. After a few moments, he opened the door. Megan received a large, warm smile when he realized it was her. "Come in, come in," he said as he beckoned her inside. "This is a great surprise, and you brought the pooch, too."

"Aww, thank you," Megan said. "You probably should be thanking Marie more than me. She made a beautiful meal the other night and made sure she packed up plenty for you to have."

Billy smiled once again. "She watches over me. She sends soups and chowders over with Tommy whenever she can catch him to bring them to me. Otherwise, she brings them herself. I had some of the leftovers after your dinner, and they were delicious."

"Now you have more of the same," Megan said as she made her way to a small table in the apartment, near the refrigerator, and began to unpack the bag. She was eager to put the food away for him, so she would get a chance to see what other fresh groceries he had available. Megan decided they would have to schedule something more formal than waiting for Tommy to be available. Now that the band was becoming more popular, he may not be around as often, and she wanted to make sure Billy was well cared for after all the years he had spent looking after Misty Manor. But Billy was proud, and he was stubborn, so she had to tread lightly. As she worked, Dudley was content to sit on the rug and watch her.

"Well, she left these things in the fridge and left orders to make sure I delivered them so here I am." Megan turned to find Billy standing behind her, eagerly watching to see what Marie had packed. "You know, she wants to start cooking again. So, I'd appreciate it if you let us bring food over more often. You'd make her very happy. She needs someone to worry after."

Billy looked at her with a strange expression on his face. "If it would make Marie happy, I'd be proud to accept her offering."

"That's great to hear," Megan said. "She'll be so happy, and you'd be making out in the deal as her cooking is fantastic." She finished placing the last of it in the fridge and turned to face him. "Would you like me to heat something for you now? Perhaps an early lunch? Some soup?"

"You got time?"

"Yes, I most certainly do. To be honest, I was hoping I could pick your brain for a moment or two about something."

"Well, then let's eat, and you can pick away."

Megan laughed as she turned back to the fridge. "Why don't you go sit in your easy chair until the food is ready and I'll put everything on the table."

For the next fifteen minutes, Megan heated food, arranged plates, utensils, and glassware to set the table. She washed the things from his cabinet which were put away with residue, probably because of dark lighting or failing eyesight. As she worked, she made a mental list of what she could buy to freshen up the kitchen and make things easier for Billy. Dudley had his head down and appeared to be sleeping in the corner.

Serving two hot steaming bowls of clam chowder, a few leftover crab cakes, and lobster rolls, Megan finally called Billy to the table. She served glasses of fresh tea poured over ice. Billy sat down and hungrily ate his meal which made her heart sad. She would put her plan in place immediately when she got home.

"So, what did you want to ask me?" Billy wiped his mouth and sat back in his chair.

"Well, I've been wondering about a lot of things," Megan started.

"Such as?"

Megan shifted in her chair as she spoke. "Well, Billy I have a few more questions about my family. You probably knew them better than I did, and I've been trying to put things together."

"I thought we did all this when we laid poor Rose and George to rest," Billy said.

"I know," Megan nodded. "But more questions have come up. A lot more."

Billy scratched his neck. "Well, I don't know what I can answer but fire 'em off, and we'll see."

Megan laughed. "Well, the first one may be easy. I happened to be at the cemetery above Misty Manor, and I wanted to know if you knew anything about the graveyard."

"You mean the one on Lighthouse road?"

"Yes, that's the one."

"What the hell were you doing way up there?"

Megan flushed as she tried to defend herself. "Billy, it's been a year since Rose died and I'm finally trying to take some control over Misty Manor and the town, but I've got to learn about it first. I'm traveling to parts of town I've never seen before, taking photos and notes. I grew up here and never noticed the view of Misty Manor from there. I know the kids screw around up there after school, but now I want to know why it's there. Who started burying bodies up there and why? You may be the only one who could tell me that."

Billy considered her question for a moment. "That may be true, I guess." He let out a long sigh. "Lighthouse Cemetery was there when I was born, but it served as a place for lost souls. It was a resting place, a potter's field, for bodies that washed up on shore. People who weren't identified or had no connections. Back when it started, I think they choose that place because they assumed a lot of the bodies were sailors lost at sea. That way, they could look out over the ocean from their eternal resting place."

"Who's supposed to be taking care of it? It's so sad because the headstones are broken, and there's garbage all over the place. The rock wall around it is crumbling."

"I don't know." Billy shrugged. "Perhaps someone in town? George used to like going up there a lot. Hell, we hung out there as kids sixty years ago. You asked about your family. Your great-grandfather, John, used to go up there on occasion as well, especially after George went missing. I guess they had a special bond there. That poor man. They were so close and spent a lot of time together. John missed that boy every day until he died, fifteen years later. Your great-grandmother, Mary, died soon after that. Her heart completely broke when George disappeared. John and Mary leaned on each other to get through that crisis, but once John died, well that was that."

Megan felt heartbroken to hear about her great-grandparents that way. She never met them, but it was one of the first times, she heard someone talk about them other than Grandma Rose, and she said very little about their personal lives and feelings. Megan didn't know much beyond their names and relationship to her.

Billy continued, "I'm glad they left Misty Manor to Rose. She had a great place to raise her son, your father, Dean Stanford. Sadly, he didn't turn out the way either of them hoped." Billy shook his head and looked at Megan. "A lot of people are jealous of the Stanford family and Misty Manor. They make assumptions about money and all, but the truth is heartbreak is a big part of the heritage of Misty Manor. Your grandmother, Rose, did a phenomenal job of instilling spirit, energy, and pride back into the place and I hope you continue the same. I feel sorry that it took so long for her to meet up with George again."

"Were there any happy times?" Megan asked, sadness flooding her face.

Billy's eyes smiled as he answered her question. "Now, don't get me all wrong. In the early years there were plenty of fun times, and parties and visitors to Misty Manor. Important visitors, too. Why, years ago, the Jersey Shore was the summer place for the President of the United States. Times have changed, but there's some mighty interesting history that happened around here in the early 1900's. There were fancy garden parties and teas." Billy leaned back in his chair, stared at the ceiling and crossed his arms. "War World II was a depressing time, but things got much better when it ended. When I think about it, things were pretty good, until George went missing."

"That's a very sad story," Megan said. "Billy, would you mind, I mean if I brought you pens and paper or a tape recorder, do you think you could tell me things you remember about my family? I know I asked the other day, but I'm serious. Maybe little interesting stories or more about all those parties you keep referring to. As you know, we didn't have many family gatherings when I was young. My great-grandparents died before I was born, and Grandma Rose shielded me from my parents who were always fighting."

Billy scrunched up his grizzled face as he thought about it, then nodded. "Yeah, I guess I could give it a try. There may be some interesting memories there. Some funny ones, too."

Megan smiled. "Thank you so much. That would be great."

"Anything in particular, you're looking for?" Billy asked.

Megan shifted uncomfortably for a moment. "If I ask you a question, can you keep it to yourself?"

Billy slapped his leg and started laughing until he had a coughing spell that wouldn't let up for several minutes. Concerned, Megan stood and tried to tap him on the back to see if that would help to break the spasm. Finally, he controlled his breathing. He looked up at Megan and said, "First of all, who am I going to talk to? You, Marie, Tommy, Nick, and Amber are the only ones who ever come by to visit. Anyway, you gonna ask me about the treasure map?"

Shock registered on Megan's face. "Yes, I was going to ask you about it."

"Well, you're not gonna be able to keep that a secret, little lady. It's been all over the internet for days," Billy said.

"You go on the internet? Is there a treasure?" Megan asked Billy.

"I didn't say that, but I've heard everyone's talking about a map. Someone is selling one on the internet."

"How could they do that?" Megan asked while shaking her head.

"Probably some fake thing they made up and the damn thing went viral, so they're playing it up for money. It would be great if we could get a look at it, though. Probably a map of someplace in Florida and everyone's too dumb to figure it out. It'll bring a lot of tourists to the town. Great marketing idea, whoever thought that up."

"To be honest, I found a lot of maps which belonged to my great-grandfather, but I can't read any of them."

"They're probably from his voyages," Billy suggested. "He was off on one of them when George went missing. Mary had gone with him which is why George stayed home to watch the house when Rose took Dean to meet her family. They all came back, and George was gone. John's days as a sea captain ended there. I think he felt guilty that if he had been home, nothing would have happened to George."

"How could he know that?"

"No one ever does, but parents worry about kids all the time."

"Billy, how would I know if one of the maps was a treasure map? Did Grandfather George or my great-grandfather ever talk about one?"

Billy thought for a moment and then shook his head. "Not that I remember. If George were on the hunt for something, he would have told me. We were tight back then and did everything together once we became friends."

Megan repeated her questions. "Well, how would you know if it were a real one anyway?"

Billy chuckled. "You've seen the ones they have for kids. You know, X marks the spot? Real treasure maps don't have that. Usually, there was a symbol that only the map maker knew about. He would put a lot of things on there to throw off anyone who might find the map by accident, but if you had a real treasure map and knew what all the symbols meant, you may be able to find a treasure."

Billy sat back again and stifled a big yawn. Megan took notice and said, "Well, I'd better be going. I'm sorry I pestered you with all these questions, but there's so much I don't know." Megan stood to clean up.

"Anytime, I enjoyed your company and the nice lunch. You tell Marie I said, thank you. I'll welcome her cooking anytime, and you can drop that paper and pen off whenever you want to."

"Thanks, Billy," Megan said as they walked to the door. Dudley followed her and waited on the stairs. Megan turned and gave Billy a quick, awkward hug. "I'll come back and see you soon."

"You do that," he said as he gave her a wink.

CHAPTER 30

egan and Dudley walked through the surf as they made their way back to Misty Manor. Looking up, she was surprised to see Nick and Teddy standing on the porch. She hurried toward the house and raced up the porch steps with Dudley behind her. Dudley immediately ran to Nick, happy to see him. Teddy, wearing an expensive suit, backed up so the dog wouldn't get hair or sand on his clothing.

"Where've you been?" Nick asked as he watched her pull out her keys.

"I went to bring some food to Billy, and we started talking. I guess the time got away from me," Megan said as she looked at her watch.

"I was starting to get worried," Nick said through a smile.

Megan opened the front door while Nick disarmed the alarm. "C'mon in, so sorry about that. It's nice to see you, Teddy."

Teddy waited until everyone was in and the dog settled. "May I?" He asked as he pointed toward the library.

"Of course, go on in. Make yourself comfortable," Megan said as she looked at Nick.

"You go in. I'll bring Dudley to the kitchen and get him a treat," Nick said as he gestured toward the library.

"Okay, thanks." Megan brushed a quick kiss against his cheek and followed Teddy.

Teddy laid his briefcase on the table and opened the latches. He was rummaging inside for papers. After finding what he wanted, he set down some documents and pulled up a chair to make himself comfortable.

Megan made her way to him and offered a quick hug about the shoulders. "How are you, Teddy? I haven't seen you in a while. Where's Jonathan? I thought for sure he'd be with you today."

Teddy's face pinched. "He's on his way back to London. Apparently, he has to handle more unfinished business over there."

"Is he planning on returning soon?"

"As far as I know," Teddy said with a frown. "So, how are you, dear?"

"Okay, I guess, but we need to meet more often. I want to start taking control of some things, but I need to know everything about the estate and Grandma Rose's plans. I've had so many questions."

"Yes, well it's been a difficult year for you," Teddy said as he covered her hand.

"You can say that again." The two turned when Nick knocked and opened the library door. "I wasn't sure if you needed me in here."

"Yes, Nick. Please come in," Megan said. "I need to talk to Teddy about all this map business and the dead body, and you'll be able to help us with that."

Nick nodded, made his way over to the table and sat down. Megan turned to Teddy. "You know there's been a lot happening. Jonathan must have discussed the secret room and this map business with you. Things have gone downhill since then, and I need to know where Misty Manor stands in all this."

"Yes, he showed me a video of the room." Teddy stopped and looked around. "It's in here somewhere?"

"Yes, right behind that bookcase over there. C'mon, I'll show you." Megan jumped up and crossed the library. She pulled the big dictionary off the end of the shelf, reached behind and pushed the lever.

They watched as the door noiselessly pulled open. Megan activated the flashlight on her cell phone and shone it inside.

"It's amazing. I was looking around the room after Nathan pointed out there was a problem. I pulled a copy of *Treasure Island* off the shelf and found the lever. Quite shocking, I would say. I grew up here and never knew that room existed."

Teddy shook his head. "Rose entrusted almost everything with me. I'm wondering if she knew about it because she never mentioned it to me."

Megan pulled the lever, and the sliding shelf closed once again. The group returned to the table and sat down.

"Nathan was very excited, and Jonathan did all he could with the video. I have no idea how we managed to be in the middle of a media circus, but I'm not happy about it."

"That makes two of us," Teddy said shaking his head.

"That makes three," Nick joined in. "The mayor has already started with Captain Davis about the reputation of the town. More tourists than ever are flocking in with this story going viral."

Teddy shot a stoic look at Nick. "Has there been a problem with that? He should be happy about increased tourism, I should think."

"True, except for a dead body who had nothing else on him except the photo of Misty Manor. We don't know yet if it was random or some plot regarding the treasure. That kind of tourism leads to a bad reputation about the safety of the town and beaches for families."

"I see," Teddy said quietly. "Do you have any information about him yet?"

"Only that he was an ex-con. We're waiting for the medical examiner to finish. I'm not sure if he was in cahoots with someone or a random perp. He does have a history of breaking and entering with intent to commit a felony. I have to go back and speak with his parole officer when he returns." Megan's eyes went wide with the news.

"So, the question remains. How did the map and story get out there?" Teddy asked, folding his hands on the table.

"The only people that initially knew were Megan, Nathan, Jonathan and me," Nick said as he looked around the table.

"Then I went to the shipwreck lecture by Doogie and asked a few pointed questions, but I didn't tell him about the map. We discussed a few things during dinner the next night, and the whole thing went wild."

Teddy shook his head. "Perhaps we'll never know. Anyone could have mentioned one thing, and the story grew from there. At any rate, we have nothing to worry about. What else came of your discussion with this Doogie fellow?"

"He's quite the historian about the Jersey Shore. He was speaking about shipwrecks and treasures. I asked him if he knew of any history about Misty Manor or the Stanford family. He said there was nothing dramatic, but then he wanted to know if we had anything historical about the house and family. I know I have nothing, so that's a big question for you, Teddy. Has anyone in the family ever started an official record that you're aware of?"

"No, I don't have anything like that. When I learned of your request, I brought copies of papers I have of birth and death dates. I have a listing of all the current properties you own." Teddy stopped fussing through the papers and looked up. "Everything I have are factual documents. I don't have any family or personal stories or mementos, but I think it would be a great idea to start a project like that." Teddy looked down and came to a decision. He looked back at Megan. "I do have the one other box I was told to keep private and safe. I was given specific instructions as to what to do with it, and I must legally follow that direction. You understand?"

Megan looked at him and shook her head. "No, I don't, Teddy. What's in the box?"

"I suppose I can tell you that. It's a box of videotapes that Rose made while you were gone. She wasn't sure if you would return and she was trying to decide what to do with Misty Manor, the trust fund and the estate. She didn't want your father to squander what the family had worked so hard to build. So, she had me draw up documents for different scenarios. One was to be used if you never returned. There was another for me to carry out if you returned and took over the trust and there was a third if you returned but didn't want any part of Misty Manor or the estate."

Megan shook her head. "I'm floored right now, Teddy. I don't even know what to say."

Teddy nodded and continued slowly. "If you hadn't returned, your father and yourself would have received a nice inheritance, and the remainder of the estate would have been turned over to charitable causes for them to completely administrate and promote. The same would have happened if you returned but wanted no part of Misty Manor. Either way, you would have had a nice inheritance, although I won't discuss details as we're not alone." Teddy looked pointedly at Nick as he spoke.

"I can go," Nick said as he went to jump up from his chair.

Megan grabbed his forearm and told him to stay. She then teared up and became angry at the same time. "Teddy, no one except you, Jonathan and I know anything about my estate, but the inheritance is the last thing I care about. I'm trying to piece my life back together from an abusive childhood, the loss of the only woman who lovingly raised me, the guilt from leaving town when I couldn't face my life anymore and doing what's right for my family namesake. I'm trying to continue all the good work my grandmother has done for this community, even though some have made it quite clear I'm not welcome. I don't give a damn about the money for my sake, and that's not what this is about."

She started to sob, and Nick put an arm around her. She leaned her head into his shoulder as he stroked the back of her hair. After a few moments, she sat up and wiped her eyes. She looked back at Teddy.

"I'm sorry," he said quietly.

"Tapes, you said Rose left tapes."

"Yes," Teddy said as he nodded his head. "They contain instructions and history about each charity, her goals for them and suggestions for what to do in the future. She didn't want me to give them to you all at once but asked me to wait until you started working with each one. Rose was afraid you'd be scared off if all this was handed to you immediately."

"Have you watched them? Are you sure they only have information about charities?"

"Out of privacy and respect, I have not watched them. My direction was to give them to you as you started each project."

Megan was silent for a moment. "Then, let's get started. Teddy, I'd like a list of each charitable organization, the members who comprise their boards and the schedule of their meetings, budgets, and activities. Once I review that, I'll set up a schedule with you for each charity and we'll move forward from there."

Teddy smiled. "Now, you're starting to sound like Rose."

CHAPTER 31

egan and Nick sat on a bench and watched the sunset over the bay. After Teddy left, they fed Dudley and Smokey, took them out for a quick walk and left the house. They stopped at one of Megan's favorite restaurants where they shared a bottle of wine and dinner. Afterward, they went for a walk along the bay and now sat on a bench at the end of a dock and watched the beautiful sunset.

"When did my life get so messed up?" Megan asked. "I swear, the harder I try to get my life together, the worse it gets."

"You're fine," Nick said as he put his arm around her. "A lot's going on right now. Concentrate on the sunset. When was the last time you saw the sunset and enjoyed the show?"

Megan snuggled against him and dreamily said, "Not in a long while. That's the point. I want to get back to watching the sunrise from the beach and swimming until I'm exhausted from the waves. I want to enjoy a great grilled burger with a cold glass of wine and lay on the porch hammock as I drift off to sleep listening to the waves."

"We're going to make sure all that happens," Nick said as he squeezed her. "You're going through a rough patch. Let's watch the bay." They sat for fifteen minutes and watched a myriad of boats and wave runners play on the water. There was a small beach on the far side of the bay where families continued to enjoy the water as the small children ran around. Someone had started a bonfire around which a group of people sat listening to someone playing the guitar.

Nick pointed out the various people on wave runners and waved to those who came close to the dock.

"Hey, I recognize those two people," Megan said as she leaned forward when a wave runner slowed near the dock.

"Ahoy, matey," said Georgie as she unclasped her arms from around Doogie's waist and waved.

"Hey, Georgie, how are you?" Megan smiled and was happy to see her friend.

Nick got up and helped to pull the wave runner close to the dock. He then offered a hand to Georgie so that she could jump off. After securing the lines, Doogie joined them on the platform and shook hands with Nick and Megan. The platform at the end of the large dock housed a bar called Pier 8800. White lights were hung over the rails and above the tables. Soft music was playing in the background as the warm weather drew crowds of visitors to relax in the moonlight.

"Hey, how are you? It's a beautiful night, isn't it?" Doogie asked as he smiled and pointed to the moon over the water.

"It's gorgeous," Megan said. "Nick and I watched the sunset. It's the first time I've come down here since Grandma Rose died. Unbelievable that tourists come from all over to see the things that some of the townspeople ignore on a regular basis."

"That is very true," Doogie said as he turned to Nick. "Hey, how about I go to the bar and get us all a couple of drinks."

"I'll go with you," Nick said as he stood up and joined Doogie on the ramp up to the bar.

Georgie took Nick's place on the bench and smiled at her friend. "How are you doing?"

"I'm okay," Megan said as her stomach clenched. "Why are you asking? Is there something else going on?"

Georgie laughed out loud. "No, but you look tired and drawn out. I thought something happened."

Megan shook her head. "Nothing other than more shenanigans with this stupid treasure map. I talked with Teddy today, and he said some things that upset me, but it's nothing I can't work out."

"I'm sorry to hear that," Georgie said as she gave her friend a hug.

"So," Megan said as she drew out the word. "It looks like you and Doogie are getting pretty cozy around each other."

Georgie looked down and blushed. "I like him. He's the first guy who gets me. There are some of us who can't leave the ocean."

"I'm glad for you," Megan said. "I hope it works out for the two of you, really I do."

"Thanks, sweetie, I appreciate it."

"So, are people still making a big deal about this treasure map?" Georgie asked with concern.

"Yes, they are, and honestly it's making me upset," Megan said as she closed her eyes.

"And it's probably a lot of angst about nothing," Doogie said as they made their way down the ramp with drinks in their hands. "For Georgie, a Summer Fizz and for Megan some Watermelon Sangria." Doogie handed them their drinks and clinked beers with Nick as they stood in front of them.

"What's the big deal with this treasure map?" Doogie asked as he looked at Nick. "I keep hearing about it. Tourists ask about it. I think they're making a new stand on the boardwalk about it. What a great idea, right? Sort of a lottery, except you have fun exploring during the hunt."

"Are you kidding me?" Megan asked after choking on her drink.

"No, I'm not," Doogie said. "I have to hand it to you, Megan. If this was a marketing ploy to bring people back to Misty Point, it was a great idea. A lot of people are looking to escape on their vacation, take a little adventure and step out of their life for a day or two. They know they won't find treasure, but they can search. It's like going on an adult ride in an amusement park."

Doogie fanned the air above him. "Misty Point, Home of Endless

Treasure." He took a long chug of his beer. "You could put a billboard right off the parkway exit."

Taking a sip of her drink, she said, "I don't think Mayor Davenport is happy about it."

"He's never happy, especially if he doesn't make all the decisions," Doogie said as he shrugged.

Megan let out a long sigh and looked at her glass. "This drink tastes delicious. What's in this?"

"It's a mixture of watermelon, Moscato wine, and rum," Doogie said. "A little too sweet for me, but others love it."

"Well, I'm certainly enjoying it," Megan said as she took another sip.

"And I like mine as well," Georgie said as she sidled up to Doogie. "Thank you very much."

"You are most welcome, ladies," Doogie said as he clapped Nick on the arm. "But Nick was with me."

"Thank you, Nick," Megan said with a smile. She then turned to Doogie. "Tell me more about shipwrecks of NJ. I want to know about the famous ones."

"Are you sure?" Doogie asked. "Once you get me started on this, I may not stop talking."

"Yes, I'd like to hear about it," Megan said as she looked at the others. "Do you guys mind?"

"No, not at all," Georgie said. "I think it would be interesting."

Nick lifted his beer to encourage Doogie to proceed.

"Okay, you asked for it," Doogie said as he pulled up chairs for himself and Nick. "We may as well get comfortable." Once Nick was settled, he began. "One of the most famous shipwrecks off the coast of New Jersey was the SS Morro Castle, which went down in September 1934. It was heading toward New York and caught fire off Long Beach Island. She wound up burning in the surf off Asbury Park. The ship traveled between New York and Cuba and gave passengers a safe place to drink during prohibition."

"Now that's interesting," Megan said as Georgie nodded beside her. "It's amazing to find people were doing a lot more than we suspected a hundred years ago. Okay, tell me another one."

Doogie nodded. "You know there are an estimated 4000 to 7000 shipwrecks off the coast of New Jersey, but I'll tell you about the most famous ones. Let's see, how about the Powhatan? She ran aground off Long Beach Island in April 1854. She was a packet ship."

"What's a packet ship?" Megan asked.

"It's a ship which delivered mail between England and the colonies. Later, it carried freight and passengers. Once again, bodies washed up all along the coast of New Jersey."

"That's kind of freaky, to think multiple bodies kept washing up," Georgie said. "I've been a lifeguard forever, and we've pulled plenty of troubled swimmers out of the waters, but we haven't had a recent shipwreck which caused a number of bodies to wash up."

"Okay, now here's an interesting one. Later, the same year that the Powhatan went down, another ship by the name, New Era, went down. It was also a packet ship, and on the way to America, several passengers died of cholera. The ship ran aground on what was known as Deal Beach but is now Asbury Park. There are rumors that passengers on that ship had diamonds and gold coins in their pockets or sewn into their clothes."

"Fascinating," Megan said as she considered his words.

"We could go on forever," Doogie said. "New Jersey has had thousands of shipwrecks off the coast. There's a Maritime Museum in Beach Haven, NJ that has records of shipwrecks from the American Revolution, as well as Navy Destroyers, German submarines, U-boats, and ocean liners. It's fascinating, you should visit one day."

"It's hard for me to realize there have been shipwrecks since the 1700's," Megan said. "We always think we're on the edge of technology and always worried about safety, but there were ships successfully crossing the ocean three hundred years ago. And who knows what cargo they had or who they were carrying as passengers? Isn't that interesting?"

"Yes, it's pretty wild to think about, and it's more than three hundred years by the way. There were ships in the 1600's as well," Doogie pointed out.

"But, it doesn't sound like any of these ships had pirates or anyone who would have hidden treasure and drawn a wordless pirate map."

"No, it doesn't," the girls agreed as they finished their drink.

Megan turned to Doogie. "Thanks for giving us all that information."

"It's the least I can do after you agreed to help us clean the beach of all that plastic. I'm looking forward to working on that project."

Megan smiled. "You got it, Doogie. Anything that makes Misty Point cleaner and a better place to live sounds like a great cause to me."

"Thanks, I appreciate that." Doogie looked at Georgie. "We'd better get going. I have to get the wave runner back before it's too late."

"Okay, I've finished my drink," Georgie said as she held up the glass.

Doogie looked at Nick. "I'm okay to drive. I never got to drink my beer, officer."

"I'm glad to hear that," Nick said. "Drunk driving is drunk driving. It doesn't matter what vehicle you're driving."

Megan and Nick walked their friends to the end of the dock. Nick held Georgie's hand as she stepped off the dock and got on the wave runner behind Doogie. He started it up and slowly drove away before he hit the throttle and gained some speed.

Megan and Nick watched until they couldn't see their friends anymore. Nick put his arm around Megan, and they slowly walked back along the bay, following the reflection of the moon in the water.

CHAPTER 32

When Megan and Nick returned to Misty Manor, they let Dudley out and walked to the edge of the ocean. They put their feet in the warm water. The pull of the surf, as well as the drink, relaxed Megan. Nick had his arm around her, and she entwined her arm around his back. It would feel nice to sit on the porch with Nick by her side. She hadn't completely committed herself to him, but she enjoyed having him with her in the house and by her side for support.

Megan returned last year to a lot of stress and confusion regarding her grandmother's illness, her childhood Grand Victorian home, her role in the town of Misty Point, as well as her inheritance of Misty Manor and all that went with it. There had been multiple controversies, and Nick had protected her and stayed by her side the whole time.

She turned to him and hugged him about the waist, and when he leaned down, she kissed him fully on the mouth. Looking forward to lying in his arms during the night, she began to pull him toward the house.

They called Dudley, and the trio began to walk toward the stairs. They stopped when they reached the porch and rested on the swing as they continued to be mesmerized by the gentle movement of the ocean as well as the warm breeze which caressed them with the scent of the salty air.

"I hope you'll be able to relax and sleep tonight," Nick said as they rocked. Megan began to feel a bit sleepy as the swing continued to move.

"I'll try to put everything aside, clear my mind and do that," Megan said as she leaned closer to Nick. "Thank you for being here and helping me work through all this."

"I'm protecting my woman," Nick said as he brushed his fingers through her hair. "It's hard work keeping you safe." He laughed as she looked up at him and frowned. "Just kidding."

She snuggled back into position and gently stroked Dudley who had jumped up on the porch swing on her other side. "I could sit out here all night. I often think of falling asleep out here, it's so relaxing."

"I'm glad to hear it, but I think you'd be better off if you went upstairs to bed."

Megan felt butterflies in her stomach. "I guess you're right, Nick." They stood up, and Dudley jumped off the swing. Together, they walked to the front door. Once Megan walked through the door, she turned and faced Nick who kissed her on the nose.

"Now make sure you lock this door tight and put the alarm code in," he said. "I'm going to stand right here and try the door before I leave."

"What?" Megan asked. "Aren't you coming inside and staying here tonight? I know you left early, but I thought your things were still here."

"I wish I could, but I've got a double shift coming up." Nick smiled and placed his forehead against hers. "Ever since they found Wade Wilton, the Captain has us doing mandatory beach patrol. Everyone is supposed to be off the beach by 10:00 p.m. He wants us to drive the beach with the searchlights and make sure there aren't any more drifters sleeping on the beach at night."

"Oh," Megan said. "I'm disappointed. I liked knowing someone was here keeping me safe."

"I think you'll be fine as long as you lock the door and put the alarm on," Nick said. "Once I'm off beach patrol, I have to go into the station. Hopefully, we'll get the coroner report tomorrow and have a little more information about Wade."

"Well, can you call me if you do?" Megan asked.

"Officially? No, I'm not supposed to tell you or anyone else anything about an active investigation."

"Whatever," Megan said as she sighed.

"Now go inside, close and lock this door so I won't have to worry while I'm at work."

"Okay, goodnight Nick," Megan said reluctantly. "I'll miss you."

"Miss you, too," Nick said as he planted one more kiss on her nose. "More than you'll ever know. Now go."

Megan laughed and called Dudley inside the foyer. She closed and locked the door and then set the alarm. She waved through the side window and watched as Nick tried the door. Then, she turned the porch light off once he had gone down the stairs.

Dudley ran into the kitchen for a drink of fresh, cool water and Megan helped herself to some juice from the refrigerator. When he heard the noise, the cat sauntered out of the laundry room after using his kitty box and stared at them.

Placing her glass in the sink, Megan waved them all forward. "C'mon, let's go upstairs and get ready for bed." The small group climbed up the grand staircase to the third floor. Megan left some of the scones lit in the halls in case she had to get up during the night.

Megan realized she was all alone in the house again. Since Marie had cooked dinner the other night, she had gone home to take care of her company. It was strange because months ago, Megan hadn't cared whether she was alone in the house and never gave it a second thought, but lately, she craved company and was thankful she had Dudley and Smokey with her.

They reached her bedroom, and the pets waited while she got ready for bed. Dudley curled up on the rug in the center of the room. Smokey walked around picking things up with his claws. He would flip something in the air and then chase it back down and pounce.

Megan undressed and tried to relax. It was a bit early to turn off the light and curiosity got the better of her, so she knelt and retrieved her ceramic bible from her favorite hiding place.

Megan sat on the bed with the ceramic Bible and carefully lifted the lid. She withdrew the yellowed paper, replaced the lid and placed the Bible on the dresser. She turned back to the bed and fully opened the map. There were many different symbols, which almost looked as if they were placed in a specific pattern. She knew there had to be a key to the symbols somewhere, but where after all these years? She had to keep looking to figure it out regardless of the outcome. She could make a few educated guesses regarding the landscape, but honestly, the coastline must have changed in the last one hundred years so who knew if any of these clues were still valid?

Shaking her head, she took the map and placed it on top of the dresser. She pulled down the covers and slipped into bed. Although it was a bit earlier than usual, it felt as if it were much later in the day. Megan was determined to rest, even if she wasn't ready for sleep. As soon as the light went out, both pets jumped onto the edge of the bed and after pulling the sheets and blankets into a comfortable position, settled themselves for the night. Megan had to pull up her legs and lean to the right to allow them the room they sought. Their situation had evolved since the first night the nervous pets arrived several weeks before last Christmas.

Megan imagined Nick driving his SUV on the beach, scanning the sand with the searchlight. Although she wanted to organize her thoughts while lying there, she hadn't planned on being in a deep sleep within minutes.

CHAPTER 33

Sunshine and morning heat poured through the oceanfront windows when Megan woke up the next morning. She sat up and rolled off the bed making her way around the pets. They jumped up when her feet hit the floor, ready to follow wherever she led. As she dressed, they reluctantly jumped off the bed and waited.

Before she left the bedroom, Megan grabbed the treasure map and put it in her back pocket. She would try to figure it out one more time or put it back into the secret room and out of her sight.

As she reached the kitchen to prepare food and drink for all three of them, her cell phone rang.

"Hello?"

"Morning sunshine," Nick said. "How are you doing today?"

"Hey, Nick. So far, I'm good, but it's early. What are you up to? How was your night?"

"I'm heading into the station for roll call. Nothing much happened on the beach. It was drizzling overnight, so everyone scattered."

"Has there been any word from the coroner?"

"I'm hoping I'll hear something when I go in this morning," Nick said.

"Okay, well let me know," Megan said.

"What are you doing today?"

"I don't know," Megan admitted. "I don't know what to do anymore."

"Why don't you relax? Stop thinking about the map and this guy for a bit. I'll take care of it. Tonight, we can grill some burgers or something."

Megan smiled as she held the phone with her left hand. She leaned against the kitchen counter and lazily stirred her cup of coffee. "What time can you be home?"

"Hopefully, I'll be there around 4:00 p.m. I pulled a double, so I should be able to leave early. In the meantime, go to the beach. Bring a book, get some sun. I don't think anything would happen during the day but be aware."

Megan picked up her coffee, turned away from the counter and sat at the kitchen table. "Maybe I'll do that, and if I do, I'll watch out," she said.

"That sounds safe," Nick said. "I'll be there soon."

"Okay, but hurry. Otherwise, I'll go out of my mind."

Nick laughed as he said, "I've got to go to work. Talk to you later. Love you."

Megan smiled and quietly said, "Love you, too."

She continued to smile as she put her cell on the table and sipped her coffee. It was supposed to be a great beach day, maybe she should sit by the water for a few hours.

Megan placed her cup in the sink and checked the laundry room in the back. She pulled out her favorite beach chair and added beach towels.

Running up the grand staircase to the third floor, she went to her room and changed into a bathing suit with a matching cover-up. The pets followed her upstairs and then ran downstairs with her as well. Megan liked Nick's idea of bringing a book, so she stopped in the library to find something she would like. Walking around the library, she read excerpts from several books before she came upon the copy of *Treasure Island* she had removed from the bookshelf to open the secret door.

Leafing through the book, she thought it was coincidental that *Treasure Island* was the title guarding the lever. She immediately resolved to read the book but realized the copy in her hands, an original first edition, was far too valuable to be reading without gloves much less on a wet sandy beach. She placed the book onto the corner of the cherrywood desk and decided to download a version on her e-reader. She placed the treasure map on the desk, under the book. Although she couldn't make heads or tails of the map, she wanted to protect it.

Walking back into the kitchen, she found suntan lotion in the pantry and loaded a bag with cold water, sunglasses, and a few snacks for her and Dudley. After petting Smokey on the head for a bit, she and Dudley went out the front door.

Dudley spent time chasing seagulls as Megan walked across the lawn to find a perfect spot on the sand. She opened and settled her chair above the high tide line, sat down and spent a few minutes slathering suntan lotion over her skin.

She sat back, put on her glasses and held her face up to the breeze. She listened to the rhythmic white noise of the waves rolling to shore and felt herself relax. Megan stretched and reached into her bag for her e-reader. She turned it on, went to the appropriate app and downloaded a copy of *Treasure Island* by Robert Louis Stevenson. She spent the next hour reading about pirates, buried gold, treasure maps, and tropical islands, and although she enjoyed what she read, it brought her no closer to understanding her treasure map. She was not able to finish the book before Dudley got restless and began running circles around her chair.

Megan got up and made her way to the water's edge with Dudley behind her. She waded until the waves crashed around her knees and took a small walk up and down the beach. She stopped at the jetty and watched the waves crash on top of the rocks. Over the years, many people had walked the jetty to be close to the waves and feel the spray of sea water hitting the rocks. Some fishermen thought they had a better catch there as well.

Megan looked down and sighed as she noticed a good amount of trash building up between the rocks. Doogie certainly had his work cut out for him. She watched as plastic cups, straws, bottles, papers, a diaper, snack bags, and cigarettes got caught, floated up when the next wave came in and then fell between the rocks when the wave receded. Megan resolved to come back as soon as possible with the things she would need to collect the trash when it floated to the surface and dispose of it properly. At least she could try to keep her little jetty clean. In addition to the trash, there was graffiti painted on the rocks. Megan stared at it and saw initials painted in hearts. She saw various names and symbols painted there and wondered how fast the paint needed to dry so it wouldn't wash away.

On one rock, she saw a symbol carved into the rock. It was a circle with a small lighthouse carved in the middle, with wiggly lines indicating rays of light coming out from its sides. Who would have carved something like this? It would have taken hours.

Megan walked to her chair. She collected her bag, folded her chair and proceeded to the house. Dudley ran behind her and then up the stairs to the front porch. Megan and Dudley followed the wraparound porch to the back door where she placed her chair against a railing. She opened the back door, so she and Dudley could get into the house. He immediately ran into the kitchen and lapped at his water bowl as Smokey ran to the kitchen to greet them. Megan was sure they were hungry and immediately reached for their food.

CHAPTER 34

*T*he station was crowded when Nick drove in that morning. After parking, he yawned with mouth wide open and scrubbed his face. He locked the car and grabbed his things before walking inside where Davis greeted him. "You look like crap."

"Thanks, Captain," Nick said. "How do you look after staying up all night combing the beach?"

"Hey, I'm way beyond that. It's good to be the captain." Davis laughed at his joke. "See anything we need to know about?"

"Nothing exciting." Nick walked toward the coffee pot before he made his way toward roll call. He found a seat on the side of the room and observed the junior officers, fresh-faced and wearing their neon shirts. They nervously talked amongst themselves but quieted when Captain Davis walked into the room and up to the podium.

"Good Morning," Davis said as he looked around the room, his face bore an unreadable expression. "You'll notice there are a few more of you on duty today. As you can see, the town is buzzing. I'm sure you're all aware of our recent murder as well as rumors of a hidden treasure. Because of the publicity, and internet coverage, we're swarming with tourists." Someone whispered in the back of the room.

A stone-faced Davis stared in that direction until several junior offi-cers turned red and looked down at their feet.

Davis cleared his throat and continued. "I want every one of you to be on your toes today. We welcome visitors but only if they obey the law. Pay attention to the crowds. Watch where they park. We don't want anyone getting hit by a car as they cross the road to get to the beach. There is no smoking or drinking on the beach. If you observe any unusual behavior, call one of your senior officers to meet you before approaching anyone. We want to keep our town safe, clean and friendly. We'll make sure they follow the rules but do it respectfully. I don't want to see any of you on the internet in an altercation with a visitor. Got it?" The group of young officers nodded their heads.

Davis reviewed some of the activities going on in town that day and asked his senior officers if they had anything to report. He checked assignments and made sure his officers knew who was assigned to the desk, parking and traffic control, bike patrol and the beach. "It's going to be hot today. Make sure you have extra water and watch for any seniors getting overheated. Our beach medics will be in their station if you need them. Any questions?"

He looked around the room for several minutes and excused the group to get to work. He rustled some papers, gathered everything up, and walked toward his office with Nick in tow.

Davis threw the papers down before he sat in the creaky chair and leaned back. He picked up his coffee cup which had been emptied hours before and never refilled.

"What's eating you?" Nick asked as he watched his boss.

"Ah, nothing but the usual," Davis said. "I think I'm getting too old for this crap."

Nick laughed. "That'll be the day. You need more coffee or sleep. When was the last time you had a vacation?"

Davis laughed. "Who can remember? Although Davenport has been trying to get me to take permanent time off."

"Our illustrious mayor," Nick said with a frown.

"Now, now, no need to be sarcastic," Davis said as he laughed again. "He's not happy your girlfriend returned to town and took away his limelight. He's narcissistic and wants everyone to know the whole world rotates around him. Besides, you're my most senior officer. Anything happens to me, you're in charge, so be careful what you wish for."

"Then we're gonna pamper you for a long while," Nick said as he spotted an envelope on the desk. "Is that the coroner's report?"

"Yeah, a courier dropped it off early this morning. I wanted to go over it with you." Davis tossed the large manila envelope toward Nick who opened it and slid out the pages. He held them up and scanned the results.

"I'm going to get some mud or whatever passes for coffee in this joint. Read through the report. We'll talk about it in a minute." Davis picked up his cup and walked out of the room, softly cursing under his breath.

Nick read the pages. The manner of death was homicide. Cause of death was exsanguination due to stab wound.

"God forbid you want a decent cup of coffee," Davis complained as he walked back in and sat stiffly at his desk.

"Something wrong with your back?" Nick asked.

Davis looked at him over the rim of the cup. "Nothing I can't take care of. Now, what did you see in that report?"

Nick glanced at the pages before him. "Guy was murdered according to this report. Looks like he was stabbed with something, but the wound doesn't match a typical knife. Coroner's not sure what the weapon was. He had other issues." Nick read parts of the report aloud. "Looks like he bled out, possibly due to liver disease. He had cirrhosis, but he may not have known. The liver was hard and nodular on the post. His heart was flabby with atherosclerosis of the arteries. Lungs showed signs of emphysema. Toxicology tests and other lab tests pending." Nick shrugged and looked up at Davis. "Looks like the typical report of a guy his age who's not taken care of himself, except the stab wound of course."

Davis grunted as he crossed his arms.

"Anything come back from forensics?"

"Nothing useful," Davis said as he shook his head. "The wind and sand obliterated most of the trace in the area. We didn't find a weapon in the area, certainly nothing with blood on it. Obviously, he wasn't alone, but it's hard to tell how many people were under that board-walk during the day, so there's no specific set of footprints. What about the parole officer?"

"He wasn't around when I went yesterday, and they didn't have the full file up. They're printing out a copy for me, but they want me to wait until a guy named Smitty is back to give it up."

"Smitty? Jeez, even I know Smitty," Davis said with a smile. "Been around for a while. He gets to know his cons and usually does a good job turning them around. He'll have something for us."

"I'm sure he'll be back at some point today," Nick said as he returned the papers to the manila envelope and on the desk.

"Make sure you get out there when you get the call from them. I want to get this wrapped up as quickly as possible. Davenport is breathing down my neck, and I want to make sure all this treasure business isn't getting anyone worked up. Damn internet blows every-thing up and turns it into a circus."

"Will do," Nick said as he pointed at the coffee. "Is that fresh?"

Davis looked at the cup. "Doesn't matter if it is. Still tastes like mud."

Nick laughed as he turned to leave the office. "I'm heading over to Stella's bakery. I'll drop you off some fresh coffee and donuts. Maybe it'll help your mood."

"That's the best thing I've heard all morning," Davis said. "Now, get the hell out there and be safe."

CHAPTER 35

Megan wiped her hands on the dishrag and watched as the two animals ate their food. She walked into the foyer and was about to get her towels and chair when she heard the phone ringing. Walking to the small table against the wall, she picked up the receiver on the old-fashioned landline. "Hello?"

"Miss Stanford?"

"Yes, you've reached Misty Manor."

"It's your mayor, Andrew Davenport." Megan groaned inwardly. At least she hoped she didn't groan out loud. She was probably the only person who would rather hear from a telemarketer than Andrew Davenport.

"Yes, how can I help you?" Megan asked and was proud she didn't add a derogatory remark at the end of her question.

"I'm responding to your inquiry. You went to town hall to ask for some documents relating to the properties you own."

"That's right," Megan said. "I'm researching the factual history of Misty Manor and the land my great-grandfather developed years ago. I'm trying to trace the history of the town." Megan had not reviewed the list of properties she owned which Teddy left with her yesterday, but it would be interesting to compare the lists. When there was silence on the phone for more than a minute, Megan hastily added. "I'm simply conducting some historical research, Mr. Davenport. There are no legalities here."

Mayor Davenport eventually cleared his throat. "I'm having the staff copy what they have here, and some of the older files are on microfiche."

"See, that's the point. I want to capture and digitize all that history before microfiche readers become extinct," Megan said but kept the sarcasm to herself. She wasn't sure, but she thought she heard a muffled chuckle from the man before he responded.

"You have every right to all the information. It will take a while to get it all to you. I'll have the office put together a packet and contact you when copies of the older documents arrive."

"I appreciate it very much."

"I do admit I was curious as to why you wanted all this information."

"And I did tell you it was for historical record keeping."

"Do I need to discuss this treasure map and murder victim with you?"

"I don't see why you would. There is no active treasure map although I understand many of the shop owners are using the theory for tourism. Also, I know nothing about the man who was murdered, much less, why. This is my town as much as it is yours, Mr. Davenport, and I also don't relish a reputation of crime or violence. Beyond that, I have nothing to tell you."

After a pause, Davenport answered her, and for once his tone was cordial. "I appreciate that. We'll leave it to the police for now."

"Sounds like an excellent suggestion."

"One more thing," he said.

"Yes?" Megan shifted position in the hall as she was getting weary with the conversation.

"You specifically asked about the cemetery on Lighthouse Road?"

"Yes, I did. I was up there doing some photography, and I didn't realize it had such a bird's eye view of Misty Manor as well as the ocean. I was interested in some of the grave markers but to be honest, the place is an eyesore, filled with garbage."

"That's interesting to hear you say," Davenport said, but almost with a lilt in his voice. "The town beautification committee has also been concerned, so we looked up the owner to speak to them about responsibility."

"And you found?" Megan said as she braced herself for what she guessed was coming.

"That the rightful owner of the property is none other than the Stanford Estate," Davenport said, almost gleefully.

Megan was quiet for several moments. "I see."

"Yes, so I'll expect you to attend to the property within, let's see, shall we say ten days to get it properly cleaned and restored. I'm sure you'll come in and apply for any necessary permits as soon as possible. I would hate to have to issue a summons."

Megan flushed but retained her composure. "If the property is mine, as you say, I'll be happy to see that it's cleaned up. I'm surprised because Grandma Rose never let anything languish, so I'm curious as to why it wasn't taken care of. At any rate, I'll be looking into it with my attorney, and you'll hear from us as necessary."

Davenport grumbled as his surprise revelation and demands were shut down. "I'll be here, you call me anytime." With that, the phone slammed down.

Megan looked at the receiver and laughed at how childish the man acted on a regular basis. And this was how the town was represented? She would look at Teddy's list immediately. Megan shook her head and turned to go back to the porch but stopped when she saw a man standing there. "You scared me. What are doing here?"

"I want to talk."

"About what? I thought Nick was clear."

"Apparently not. You left the back door wide open, so I figured it was an invitation to come inside."

"Well, you thought wrong." Megan fumed and started to walk around the man when he put his arm out to the side.

"Not so fast," he said.

"How dare you? Get your hands off me." Her raised voice and terse tone alerted Dudley, and he immediately began to bark. Megan looked up to see the door to the kitchen was closed.

"Oh, I forgot to mention I closed the door while you were on the phone. The dog's fine, but he won't be available until after we speak."

"What do you want?" Megan asked realizing he wasn't about to go away.

"What else? I want the treasure map."

"The map again. I wish we never found it. We don't even know if there's a treasure!"

"Well, we're going to do our best to find out, and the key must be part of the map. There may be invisible ink or something else, but I need the original map."

Megan was speechless. "How in the world do you think you're going to get away with this?"

"I'll have enough of a head start, no one is going to find me. When I figure out where the treasure is, I'll either dig it up or have someone help me. C'mon let's go," he said as he waved her towards the library.

"Where are we going?" Megan asked, confused.

"I'm assuming the map is still in the library."

"What if I refuse?" Megan asked.

The man opened his jacket far enough for Megan to see a gun.

"You're going to shoot me?"

"No, probably not, but I can't promise anything about your dog. Even if I were convicted, I'd get nothing but a fine and a slap on the wrist. You want to challenge me on that?"

Megan's mouth fell open as she struggled with emotions.

"Let's go, show me where the map is."

Megan turned in the foyer and led him to the library. She walked across the room and looked down at the desk. She hesitated for a moment and then heard Dudley barking in the kitchen. She quickly pulled the map out from under the book, turned around and handed it over.

He took a moment to open the map and look it over. Satisfied it was the same map, he waved at Megan. "Okay, now open the door to the room."

She cocked her head and stood still. "Why? I gave you the map, now go."

"I appreciate that, but I said I needed a head start. Turn around and let's go." He pushed her toward the bookshelf. "Open it up."

Standing so close that he was breathing down her neck, he watched as she took the dictionary off the shelf and reached behind to push the small lever. The shelf moved noiselessly and revealed the opening to the secret room. Once it was open, he stood behind her and breathed into her ear. "Ladies first." Megan didn't turn around as she couldn't bear for her face to be close to his. She took a tentative step forward and waited for him to follow her. Instead, he shoved her forward, and she fell on the floor. He quickly backed out of the room, closed the bookshelf and replaced the dictionary.

"Hey," Megan screamed. "Hey, let me out of here." She stood up and put her hands out to steady her position. Once the bookshelf was in place, the windowless room was pitch dark. She stood for a moment, trying to get her bearings as her heart hammered in her throat. She listened very carefully, but the sound was muted by the walls and numerous books lining the shelves. She took a few tentative steps, much like a baby starting to walk. A wide-based gait with hands held out to the side to keep her from bumping into unknown objects. She slowly made her way to where she thought the opening would be. She put her hand forward, hoping to feel a piece of wall. Eventually, her fingertips landed on wood on some sort, and she started to knock on the door.

"Hey, let me out. This isn't funny." She continued to knock on wood until her fingers ran into something gauzy and she realized it was a spider's web. She immediately pulled her hand back, but fibers stuck to her fingers like cotton candy at a carnival. She pulled her hand close to her chest and started to feel the walls closing in.

She couldn't tell if there were bugs in the room and she was afraid to move. The room suddenly felt stuffy, and she longed for cool, fresh air. The ocean breeze, a fan, or the cold breeze of an air conditioner. There were no windows. What if there was no fresh air? How long did she have in there before someone searched for her?

Fingers shaking, she pulled the cell phone out of her back pocket. Chiding herself for panicking, she opened the phone, her fingers fumbled as she tried to dial. Nothing happened. Checking the phone, there was no signal inside the room.

"C'mon, c'mon, think," she told herself as she wondered what to do. She opened her phone again and hit the flashlight icon. Breathing a sigh of relief, the light went on, and she was able to orient herself in the room, although it looked surreal with the small light breaking through the inky darkness. She slowly turned and saw the table with the mariner's display. She looked for anything that would help her get out but found nothing that would serve as a tool or allow her to signal help.

Taking a deep breath and feeling very flushed, as well as slightly dizzy, she made her way over to where she thought the opening should be. Holding the light with one hand, she prodded with her fingertips to find a lever or latch on the inside of the room which would open the door. She slid her fingers down what she thought would be the seams, but the door was recessed away from the room, and she connected with nothing useful.

Her legs began to shake, her feet were sweating, and she continued to feel hot and faint. She felt a small vibration in her hand and looked down in dismay to see words on the screen,

Low Battery, Power less than 10%.

Megan wasn't sure how much power the flashlight drew from her phone, and she couldn't remember when she charged it last, but certainly before she went to the beach.

Feeling confused, she couldn't think straight, and her legs shook even more. To save a little bit of power, she turned off the phone and began pounding on the wall. She stopped and waited a few more minutes but heard nothing. She began to cry, her heart raced as panic fully set in. She pounded more furiously on the wall until her knuckles were scraped and raw. Shaking, she stopped and sunk to the floor.

CHAPTER 36

$\mathcal{N}$ ick finished his sandwich, balled up the wrapper and threw it at the rear windshield in a backward overhand motion. He felt sleepy due to the double shift but regained some energy after drinking a large caffeinated soda and eating lunch.

He was leading beach patrol today, making sure the junior officers were able to carry out their duty safely. He spent the day observing people fighting over parking, sneaking cigarettes and alcohol onto the beach, gaining access without beach badges, fighting over prime beach spots, jaywalking, driving with cell phones and becoming the focus of beach emergencies. He could never figure out how people thought sitting in 100-degree weather with a hangover would be beneficial to one's health. Already dehydrated from the alcohol, the sun continued the process until they passed out from heat stroke.

Nick sat in his cruiser for lunch and was happy to take advantage of the air conditioner while he watched the crowd in front of him migrate toward the water. Thank goodness the morning water test was clear of bacteria. The water quality was becoming more of an issue every year.

He frowned when his cell phone went off. "Hello?"

"Nick? It's Edna at the station."

"Hey, Edna. What's up."

"You got a call. I tried to tell the guy you weren't in today, but he insisted I patch through to you. Said you'd want the call."

"What's his name?"

"I have it, hold on a moment." Nick listened as Edna shifted through some papers.

"Here it is. Said his name is Smitty."

Nick straightened at the wheel. "Smitty? Yeah, I need to speak with him. Edna, put him through."

"You got it," she said, already transferring the call.

When he heard the ring, Nick picked up the phone. "Officer Taylor."

"Hey, Smitty here, from the county jail."

"Thanks for calling me back," Nick said as he lowered the air conditioner blower in the car.

"What can I do for you?"

"I'm looking into a murder we had in town. An ex-con, who was followed by you. Wade Wilton. I'm looking for some info on the guy."

Smitty snorted in the phone. "I know him well. He's had a couple runs with us. I have his complete file on my desk if you want to come down and look through it."

"Yes, when can I do that?"

"I'm here all afternoon if you want to swing by," Smitty said. "Come on in, I'll set up a desk somewhere, so you can see if anything lights up."

"Great, I appreciate it," Nick said. "I'm on my way over."

Nick put the SUV in gear, called the station to get someone to cover the rest of his shift and headed toward the county jail.

CHAPTER 37

Megan sat on the floor and wiped her sweat covered
forehead. Her breathing had calmed a little, but her
heart continued to race. She remembered there was a chair in front of
the small desk, so she reached out with her fingertips until she
connected with something and kept a tight grip until she was able to
stand up. She pulled her cell phone out, hoping she had enough juice
to use the flashlight to reorient herself in the room. Thrilled with a
small amount of light, she spied the chair, inched over to it and sat
down. Dreading the moment, she turned the flashlight off to save as
much battery as she could. She sat back and closed her eyes even
though the room was pitch dark to channel her other senses. Taking a
deep breath, she tried to relax and think.

Megan listened carefully, and although she couldn't hear much,
she thought she heard Dudley barking in the kitchen. She wasn't sure
if anyone heard her when she was knocking on the door and she
knew, by now, there was no one in the house to help her. She tried to
concentrate on whether she felt a small draft to indicate any fresh air
in the room, but she didn't think so. Opening her eyes, the room
seemed less dark, but there was no obvious source of light.

She continued to sweat in the airless room, although she wasn't sure if it was from heat or anxiety. She closed her eyes once again and tried to remember everything she had seen in the room. She mentally scanned the room, hoping there was something which would help her escape before it was too late.

CHAPTER 38

*N*ick pulled into the parking lot of the county jail, called in his location and went inside. He tried to call Megan several times on the way over to let her know they may get a break, but her phone went right to voicemail. Nick wasn't sure if she had gone to the beach, but he left a message each time to have her call back.

Walking into the small waiting room, Nick approached the counter and asked for Smitty. The officer behind the desk told him to wait until he called Smitty to let him know he had a visitor.

Nick scanned the room, noting most of the furniture was nailed down. There were no loose items on the counter. No sense supplying an ex-con with a weapon or something he could use in a violent situation.

A balding gentleman, with a wide waistline and a crew cut, walked out from an office and up to the counter. "Taylor?" He offered a smile with his hand.

"Yes," Nick said as he walked over. "Thanks for calling me."

"C'mon back to my office so we can talk." He pushed a buzzer, so Nick could raise the counter and pass through. Once the counter was closed, they walked down a small hallway lined with faded carpet. The old-fashioned paneled walls held faded paper photos attached with tape.

They entered an old battered office, and Smitty indicated a chair for Nick to sit while he went around the desk and settled into his own chair. Smitty pulled papers aside and pushed a thick manila folder to the center of his desk. He opened it, leafed through papers, closed it and pushed the whole thing over to Nick.

"So, what exactly happened?" Smitty asked as he watched Nick start to scan the papers in front of him.

"We're not sure. We got a call about a dead body under the boardwalk. Prints led back to your guy. He had no identification, but he had a photo of a Grand Victorian from Misty Point by the name of Misty Manor."

"Oh," Smitty chuckled. "Is that the place with the hidden treasure?"

Nick looked up. "That's the rumor going wild, although we have no direct knowledge of such."

"How did you say Wade died?"

"It appears he was stabbed to death. Not a regular knife so I'm not sure what the actual murder weapon was. We're trying to get a line on whether he had friends in Misty Point. I don't know if he had any plans about Misty Manor or if he happened to hear the rumors. I'm trying to establish some connections."

"I get it," Smitty said as he nodded his head.

"You knew this guy better than anyone, I suppose," Nick said as he continued to turn pages. "What was he like? Who did he hang with? Any family or connection to our town?"

Smitty leaned back in his chair and scratched his head for a moment. "Wade was a frequent guest, but he was all about small misdemeanors. Some breaking and entering, petty theft, stuff like that. He wasn't into drugs. He was pretty strict about that ever since his little sister died from a heroin overdose."

"What about cell mates?"

Smitty shrugged. "Nothing to write home about. Some fights in the cell. He had no gang affiliation, so he wasn't loyal to anyone. He didn't have any regular visitors, no family I know of at this point, and his attorneys were all public defenders so no one with a permanent connection."

"Was he looking for trouble when he left?"

"No, and that's why I was surprised when you called. Every time he was in, we set him up in a community program. At first, he resisted like everyone else and blew it off, but after a while, he looked forward to it. To be honest, the last time he came through, I almost felt he purposely committed a crime so that he could get hooked up again. He was learning a trade and could have been a good mentor to other inmates, so I'd be surprised to learn he left here looking for a big score. Much more likely, someone was trying to pull him in."

"And no one around him seemed connected to a beach town?"

"Not that I know of, but you got the whole file right there. I can't let you take it with you, and we're not on computers yet, so I can't print anything out, but you can read until your heart is content and see what you find."

Nick nodded. "Okay if I take notes?"

"Sure, don't take original documents." Smitty stood up. "Excuse me, but I gotta go to the can. I'll be back to check on you."

"Thanks, appreciate it," Nick said as he continued pawing through each page.

Nick continued to turn pages, read names and reports of Wade's activity while in jail and community programs. He didn't recognize anything which would connect Wade Wilton to Misty Point or Misty Manor. He had almost finished with the folder when Smitty came back into the room, holding a donut.

"Find anything?" Smitty asked with food in his mouth. He used the donut to point into the hall. "They got more food out there if you're hungry."

Nick held his hand up. "No thanks, I'm good."

Smitty sat down at the desk as Nick turned the last page. "Sorry, it didn't work out for you."

"Hey, thanks for the info. I have some notes in case something comes up on my end, I can collaborate from there."

As Nick went to push the folder back toward Smitty, some of the papers and a few photos flew out of the back. Nick picked up the papers. "Hey, what are these?"

"Oh, sometimes we take photos of graduation ceremonies or special events for the community programs."

"That's nice." Nick pushed the papers forward but held back a photo. His eyes opened. "Holy crap."

"Find something?" Smitty asked.

"Tell me about this photo? Do you have any more information?" He handed it to Smitty who turned it around and looked at it.

"Oh, that was a special event surrounding a program we had for ex-cons to learn a trade. It was a carpentry session. The cons assembled special pieces of wood into things for a children's park." Smitty looked at the photo a little more closely. "I think this was a wooden pirate ship that was going to some beach." Smitty handed the photo back to Nick. "Recognize anyone specific?"

"I sure as hell do," Nick said as he pulled his cell phone. "Can I take a pic of this?"

"It was a public photo, so I don't see why not."

Nick snapped a pic of the photo. "Thanks, I've got to go." He pushed everything toward Smitty, shook his hand and headed out the door while trying to get Davis on the phone.

Smitty looked down at the photo. He saw a smiling Wade Wilton with a certificate in one hand and two men beside him. One had his hand on his back, while the other stood nearby. The description on the photo said, "Community program benefits children's park.

Pictured left to right, Wade Wilton, Mayor Andrew Davenport, Nathan Graham."

Smitty grunted and placed the photo back into the folder.

CHAPTER 39

ick sat in the cruiser and texted the photo to Davis. He put the car in drive and called Megan's cell. He wanted to tell her what he found to warn her. No answer. He redialed the phone with the same result. Normally, she was very responsive to her phone. He had texted her several times during the day with no response. She may not be able to make a call if she were near the water, but she should have received his text messages. Fear gripped him as he realized something must be wrong. He flipped on the lights and sirens and dialed Davis.

"Did you get the photo I texted you?" Nick asked as he drove with one hand down the two-lane road.

"I sure as hell did," Davis said. "Interesting the mayor is barking up our ass when he's had more exposure to the guy than any of us."

"I've been trying to reach Megan all day with no answer, and now I'm getting worried," Nick said, as he made a turn faster than he should have.

"I'll send Peters over to Misty Manor," Davis said. "And I'll be happy to walk across the hall to have a little chat with the mayor."

"Okay, I'm ten minutes out, but send Peters now. Something's wrong. I can feel it."

"I'm on it," Davis said. "Try not to run into a wall, will ya?"

Nick shook his head and hung up the phone. He tried to call Megan again with no answer. He clicked off the cell phone and turned the corner toward Ocean Ave. He skidded into the driveway at the same time Peters came from the front of the house.

"Everything looks normal, but no one is answering the door," Peters said.

"Okay, I'll take the back." Nick ran around the back of the house. He saw Megan's car parked by the garage, so he knew she wasn't far. Popping up onto the wraparound porch he saw the sandy beach chair against the railing and the back door wide open.

Peters joined him on the porch. They knocked on the door and shouted "Misty Point Police." No one answered, but Dudley started barking and scratching the kitchen door.

Nick turned to Peters. "That's not normal. She never locks the dog in the kitchen when she's home alone." Remembering the last time he and Davis caught someone in the kitchen with a knife, Nick said, "Let's go in, but don't let the dog out until we know what's going on."

"You got it," Peters said softly, holding his gun.

Nick pulled his gun, nodded to Peters to take the other side of the doorway and slowly moved past the door to look inside. "Misty Point Police."

Nick saw nothing unusual in the kitchen except for Dudley barking and running toward him. He stepped inside the kitchen and nodded toward the laundry room. Peters went over and looked inside. They found nothing there.

Davis appeared at the back door as the two officers came out of the kitchen. "What's going on?"

Nick shook his head. "Something's off. We have to clear the house."

"This is a pretty big house," Peters said.

"I'm going to the third floor," Nick said. "I want to check Megan's bedroom and make sure there's nothing wrong."

"I'll take the second floor," Davis said as he turned to them. "Peters, you take the first floor."

The officers dispersed to check the rooms and house. Nick ran up to the third floor and quietly down the hall until he reached Megan's bedroom. He stood to the side of the door and pushed the door open to look inside. He didn't see anything unusual. The bed was made. There were a pair of jeans and a shirt on the bed. He didn't find anyone or any evidence of a struggle. Nick cleared the rest of the rooms on the third floor and went to help Davis on the second.

When the second floor was cleared, they headed to the first floor. Peters was in the foyer and shaking his head to show he hadn't found anything. When Nick reached the foyer, Dudley heard his voice and barked furiously. Nick went to check on him, and when he opened the kitchen door, Dudley ran up and jumped on him, the dog then turned and ran out of the kitchen. Within seconds, he returned to Nick and did it again, but this time ran into the library, barking loudly. Nick turned to Peters who shrugged and said, "I didn't see a damn thing in there."

"I believe you, but this is Misty Manor, and there are things you don't know about." Nick ran into the library and found Dudley in front of the bookshelf, barking madly.

"What the hell's up with that dog?" Davis asked.

Nick quickly pulled a couple of books off the shelf. He reached behind, found the lever and pulled the secret door open. As he did so, Megan's body, which was leaning against the door near the floor, fell out into the library.

"Holy smokes," Peters said as he and Davis watched Nick drop to the floor to check Megan. Nick shouted Megan's name as he placed his shaking fingers against her carotid artery. "She's alive." He felt a weak pulse and warm air leaving her mouth when she breathed. He quickly checked her over but didn't see any blood or bruises. Patting her cheeks, he wiped the sweat off her forehead and brushed her wet plastered hair away from her face.

Behind him, Davis was on the radio calling for an ambulance. "Is she with us?"

"She's breathing. She must have gotten locked in the room without any fresh air."

"Damn good thing you knew about the room," Davis said sarcastically. "We'll talk about that later."

Peters had gone to the kitchen and returned with a cool rag.

As Nick wiped her head and neck, Megan's eyelids fluttered open. She looked up to see Nick kneeling over her and smiled before she started sobbing.

"You're okay," he said as he leaned down to hug her. "We found you, you're safe."

She only said one thing as the ambulance siren wailed. "It was Nathan. Nathan Graham."

CHAPTER 40

$\mathcal{M}$egan leaned back and looked around the trauma room. Nick stood silently by the gurney and held her hand.

"This is the second time you've been in this room in six months," Nick said as he raised his eyebrows. "The place gives me the creeps, so please stop."

"It's not exactly like it was my choice," Megan said as the ER doc walked into the room. Dr. Curtis Jeffries was an attractive African American gentleman with dreadlocks and a great personality. Always grinning, he had a special demeanor for working in an area of the hospital which constantly brought dread and fear to those who visited.

"Ah, Miss Stanford, you wanted to come to my ER and see me again?" He laughed as he tilted his head back.

"Well, I'd rather it was under different circumstances," Megan said, feeling herself relax in his presence.

"I don't know," he teased. "Perhaps you had too much fun last time?"

"No offense, Dr. Jeffries, but I don't think so."

"Then I must let you go. I looked at your tests, and they are all fine. I think you were anxious and overheated. You need to go home, drink a lot of fluids and rest." Dr. Jeffries looked at Nick standing near the gurney and said, "Perhaps this fine officer would be willing to take you home and look after you." He then smiled at Megan and offered a wink before he turned to Nick. "It's good you are a trained officer because I fear the will is strong with this one." Megan squinted with one eye as Nick chuckled.

"The nurse will come in and help you dress and collect your paperwork. The next time I would like to see you is at the grocery store. Try not to come back to my ER, but I will be here if you must." Dr. Jeffries shook Megan's hand in his large warm one and smiled. "Take care of yourself, Miss Stanford."

"Yes, I plan to," Megan said a little too emphatically.

They watched Dr. Jeffries leave and waited until the nurse walked in. "I'll go out to the hallway," Nick said. "Davis is out there, and I'm sure he'll have questions, but I'm waiting for you."

"Okay, let's get out of here."

Nick left the room, and the nurse helped Megan to stand. She watched Megan to make sure she wasn't dizzy and then handed over her clothing so that she could change. Once she was dressed and ready to go, the nurse reviewed a set of discharge instructions as well as the proper follow-up information. Megan thanked her and tucked the paperwork into her purse. The nurse had her sit in a wheelchair so that she could push her out to the ER discharge area. Megan was wheeled to the curb where the police cruiser was waiting. They helped her into the car as several people watched. They all looked to see if she was in handcuffs.

"Thanks for the ride," Megan said. "The bystanders all assume I've been arrested."

"I'm not sure I'd rule that out yet," Davis said, turning red from the neck up. "When we get back, I'll be asking for a few details of what happened today."

"I'm the victim," Megan said. "There's nothing to arrest me for."

Davis growled. "Maybe, I'll think of something."

Megan laughed. "You're starting to sound like Davenport now."

Davis chuckled as they drove toward Misty Manor. They pulled into her driveway, and Nick walked her up to the house. Davis had checked in with Edna to make sure nothing was pending at the station that couldn't be handled by the other officers. Reassured, he turned off the car and walked up to the house.

The back door was open for Davis who found Nick and Megan in the kitchen. Dudley came running to make sure everything was okay. Megan was sitting at the table, and Nick was getting her a large glass of iced tea. Davis pulled out a chair, the legs scraping the floor as he pulled. He sat down as Nick leaned back against the counter and crossed his arms.

"There are some things you need to fill me in on," Davis said, storm clouds gathering in his eyes. "I need to know everything, especially if it's related to this murder."

Megan flicked a glance at Nick. "Why don't you start the story with the day we found the room?"

Nick nodded. "Okay. About a week ago, Nathan Graham and Megan were looking at original blueprints of Misty Manor. She had hired him on a recommendation from Teddy Carter. He noticed the blueprints were off. I happened to be there that day. We searched the room, and Megan found a bookshelf which opened into a secret room. There was no light, but we got together a couple of days later to check it out." Nick turned to Davis. "You remember when I borrowed the emergency lighting." Davis nodded.

"Anyway, we found a lot of things in there including a safe with a small treasure chest, a piece of jade and a map. Nathan Graham went nuts over it. He kept coming back because he was convinced there was a fortune hidden somewhere."

"That's how all this treasure stuff got started?" Davis asked as he glowered at them. "Why didn't you tell me this?"

Megan shrugged. "I didn't think there was anything to it."

"You didn't?" Davis took a deep breath while he reached into his pocket for his pad and a pen. "Okay, so tell us what happened today."

"Nothing short of ordinary," Megan said. "I went to the beach with Dudley to read. When I came back, I left my chair on the porch and fed the animals. Then the phone rang. It was Davenport giving me grief about some information I requested at town hall. When I hung up and turned around, Graham was standing behind me demanding the treasure map. He walked me into the library and locked me in the secret room."

"You're damned lucky he didn't kill you outright," Davis said.

"Teddy recommended the man," Megan said. "I assumed he wasn't dangerous."

"But he's had contact with a lot of ex-cons. Graham ran a community program to rehabilitate prisoners jailed for misdemeanors, so he had plenty of opportunities to connect with people." Nick brought the photograph of Wade Wilton, Nathan Graham, and Andrew Davenport up on his cell and handed it to Megan.

"That scum," Megan said. "Are they both in on it? Did Davenport distract me while Nathan did the dirty work?"

Davis shrugged. "That's unknown for now. I talked to Davenport as soon as Nick sent me the photo, but he denied knowing him. According to Davenport, he's a popular and well-loved politician who's had millions of photo-ops with people so there's no way he could know each one personally."

Megan frowned as she took a drink of water. "So, now what?"

"We look for Graham. I put out a BOLO. The man has a business nearby, and if he's looking for treasure, he's not going anywhere," Davis said.

"I think I'll put a call out to Teddy and see if he has any other contact information we could use. I also want to see how he knows him," Nick said.

Megan eyes filled with tears. "I'm so sorry about all this. I can't believe this escalated into a ridiculous situation."

Nick threw an arm around her and pulled her close. "The only thing we need to do is figure out a way to reign it in."

Megan nodded. "I have an idea about that."

Davis stood up and jammed his hat on his head. "I'm going. Megan, feel well and be very careful. Nick, I'll see you at the station in the morning."

Nick nodded. "I'm staying here for the night. Megan needs to get some proper rest, and I'll make a few calls in the meantime."

CHAPTER 41

The next morning, Megan sat at the kitchen table and sipped a strong cup of coffee. Dudley and Smokey sat at her feet while Nick puttered around the kitchen. "Hey, you're getting pretty good at this."

Nick laughed. "I'm going to have to stay here more often to protect you. How are you feeling?"

"I've got a headache, and I feel tired and sore, but otherwise okay."

"You should rest today and drink plenty of fluids. You were dehydrated and overheated when we found you. Your friend here was the one who found you." Nick pointed to Dudley. "We cleared the house, but then he jumped me and ran into the library. He wasn't taking 'no' for an answer. Thankfully, I knew about the room. If I hadn't been here, the other officers wouldn't have checked any further."

Megan reached down and hugged Dudley as hard as she dared. "He wouldn't leave my side last night. That's the second time he's saved my life. I don't know how I ever survived without him and Smokey."

As if the cat knew she mentioned him, he started to swirl about Megan's legs as she sat at the table.

Nick pulled out a chair and sat with his cup of coffee. "Dudley's been amazing since you rescued him last Christmas. He's a great dog. I'm thinking about talking to Davis about starting a K-9 team in Misty Point. I need to find out more of what it takes to train the dogs and pick a good officer, but he's been very helpful."

"He would have taken out Graham if he hadn't been locked in the kitchen," Megan said as she continued to stroke his head. "Poor doggy."

Everyone looked up when the doorbell rang. Nick looked at his watch and then quickly back at Megan. "I have a confession. I'm leaving for the station, so I called Georgie and Amber to see if they could spend time with you this morning. Hate me if you want, but I don't want you to be alone."

Nick got up and went to the front door with Megan, Dudley, and Smokey following behind. After opening the door, Georgie and Amber pushed in with bags of bagels, donuts, coffee, and juice. They put them down on the table in the foyer and rushed over to Megan. Nick watched as they hugged her. "Oh honey, I can't believe what happened to you. We're staying right here today. Marie's company left so she's coming to stay here for a while as well."

Megan closed her eyes, grateful for Nick, Dudley, her friends, and Marie. She kissed Nick goodbye as he went to work, turned to her friends and said, "Okay, I'm starving, let's eat."

The day passed uneventfully. They ate breakfast in the solarium while watching the ocean. The ocean breeze cleared any leftover haze from the day before. Megan repeated the story to her friends and continued to hug Dudley throughout the day. Marie arrived loaded with bags of food and began to make dinner for anyone who happened to be at Misty Manor when the time came.

"Hey, do you mind if Doogie comes over?" Georgie asked as she poured a glass of wine for each of them while they sat on the porch. "Marie said there's plenty of food for dinner."

"Fine with me." Megan picked up her glass and only took a sip. "Nick called, and he's staying late to follow up on some leads, so he won't be here."

"Tommy won't be able to come. He's going to visit Billy this afternoon and then straight to a rehearsal for the concert, which is so exciting," Amber said while shaking her head. "I won't see him much until it's over, but it's still very exciting." She looked over at Megan. "Don't forget we have front row tickets and we'll be backstage the rest of the time. I hope your headache is gone by then."

"I'm sure it will be," Megan said with a smile.

"Great," Georgie said as she texted Doogie to come to Misty Manor.

"So, go to the beginning and tell us about the map again," Georgie said. "I know you brought it up to Doogie at dinner, but maybe if we see the whole picture? At this point there's more speculation than fact, so you might as well spill."

Megan finished her drink, waited for Doogie and then went over the story again. She described in detail the bookshelf and how she removed the original copy of *Treasure Island* to open it. She described the map and took out her tablet. "Here, I took full photos of the map. Obviously, I don't have the original anymore but here's a copy. I can't make heads or tails of it. There are a lot of symbols but nothing that lends itself to a specific trail."

"Did you go through the book?" Doogie asked.

"You mean *Treasure Island?*"

"Yes, maybe, as you said, it was there for a reason."

"I almost read the entire story when I was on the beach yesterday, but there was nothing there that seemed to give a clue."

"Maybe it's not the story," Doogie said. "Maybe it's the book itself. Did you leaf through it carefully?"

Megan paused. "I didn't because the book is 135 years old. It's a first edition published by Cassell & Co in 1883. Before that, the story was serialized in a children's magazine. I'm not a book conservator, but I think I should find one to give me some tips."

"Well, maybe we should look through it," Doogie suggested. "You'd be the only one to touch the book," he added when he saw Megan's face.

"I had to look into antique books at work," Amber said. "I know you have to be concerned with humidity and how you handle the spine."

"And wear gloves," Georgie said. "I think you have to wear white cotton gloves, but I'm not positive."

Megan laughed. "I do remember that you can't let the book open completely. I know you're supposed to let each side rest on something soft to decrease the opening angle."

"C'mon," Doogie said. "No one will touch the book, but let's try it. Maybe we'll find the key to the whole mystery there."

Megan nodded. "Okay, let's go." The group followed her into the library and sat at the table while she retrieved the original copy of *Treasure Island*. She sat at the end of the table and followed everything they could think of to protect the book. They placed the book on a soft cushion and didn't let the pages fully open. Megan made sure her hands were clean, but she didn't have white gloves. Proceeding very slowly, she turned the pages one at a time gazing at the writing without reading the actual story.

"It's amazing how different books look today than they did a hundred years ago," Megan said as she continued to scan.

"There's a lot more space on the page now than back then. They used to jam a lot of text on one page."

Megan chuckled but then stopped as she came near the end of the book, she found a yellowed scrap of paper with fancy faded blue writing. "Look what I found."

"What is it?" The group crowded around her, trying to see. Megan took the paper and laid it carefully on the table. Before she did anything else, she took a photo with her cell phone. Then leaning forward, she read the faded scripted writing.

"It says, *'This key will find the treasure.'* There's a symbol here, and I recognize it as one of the symbols on the map," Megan said excitedly.

Doogie looked at the photo she had taken. "You know, very often that's all that was placed on a map. The symbol under which one would find a treasure. The rest is subterfuge to lead other's away from the actual treasure. The key is to know the right symbol."

"I can't believe it, but I saw that symbol yesterday," Megan said.

"While I was on the beach with Dudley, we went for a walk near the ocean's edge, and I climbed onto the jetty. I saw this symbol carved into one of the rocks on the jetty."

"Maybe that was the first step to show it was the right beach," Doogie said.

"The rest of the map seems to focus on a lot of places," Georgie added.

"Yes, but lighthouses are more frequent," Doogie said. "And that's a lighthouse in the middle of the symbol."

"What year was the lighthouse built?" Amber asked Megan.

"I don't know exactly but somewhere around the same time as Misty Manor which is early 1900's. The problem is I don't know if the map preceded the lighthouse or not. I saw that myself and I took a trip to the cemetery on Lighthouse Road hoping to find something there."

"Jeez, that place is a mess. I can't believe you went there by yourself," Georgie said. "Did you find anything?"

Megan made a face at Georgie. "As you said, the place is a mess. Headstones were toppled over, garbage was strewn about. I wasn't aware, but there's a bird's eye view of everything that happens at Misty Manor. I checked town hall to find some history on the cemetery, and that's one of the things Davenport called me about yesterday. To inform me the cemetery is on Stanford property and then threaten me with legal action if I didn't clean it up. I swear he was laughing at the time."

"Very interesting," Doogie said as he looked at his watch. "It's late afternoon, but we have time before dinner. Let's take a run up there and look around. If we find that symbol on one of the headstones, we can...,"

"What? Dig it up?" Amber cut him off mid-sentence. "Are you getting treasure fever, too?"

"No," Doogie said crossing his arms defensively. "Just trying to help out here."

Georgie stood between Amber and Doogie. "Stop. Let's be friends. We don't need any more arguing over this stupid treasure. My grandmother used to say things like this were all over blood money anyway."

Megan looked down and closed the book. "Listen, why don't you let me look into it? I don't want to cause any more problems."

"No," Georgie said. "We'll go as a group. Let's look at the head-stones and see if we find a symbol. While we're there, we can size up how to fix the place."

"And hope we don't run into anyone we don't know," Megan said sadly.

CHAPTER 42

Doogie pulled the car to the side of the road and turned off the engine. The group looked at the small cemetery surrounded by the crumbling rock wall. Weeds and wild growth covered toppled headstones. Garbage lined the rock wall, and graffiti lined the posts.

"What a mess," Megan said. "I don't remember my family ever mentioning this place as I was growing up."

"I remember it from high school," Amber said. "Admit it, everyone hung out here to drink or make out at some point."

"Not everyone," Georgie and Megan said in unison.

"Who does the big marker in the middle belong to?" Doogie pointed out the side window of the car.

"I have no clue," Megan said. "I looked around briefly, but I had no idea what I was looking for. I don't remember any names either. I was told this cemetery was for sailors who died and remained unclaimed. They were buried here to make sure they had a great view of the sea. Let's look around a bit. We can split up the cemetery and check each headstone. If anyone sees this symbol, yell out so we can mark the spot."

Megan took her cell phone and texted a photo of the symbol to everyone in the car. The group approached the rusty gate and headed to the large monument. It was approximately six feet high and dedicated to all the unnamed souls who had been lost at sea. It was dated 1915.

"I don't see any names or symbols on the monument," Megan said.

"Neither do I," Doogie agreed.

"We have no idea who's buried here or when the last burial was held. I imagine there must be a record somewhere, but if there aren't any names, that won't be helpful."

"Okay, everyone take a corner, check all the headstones and meet back at this monument. There can't be more than a hundred people here, so it should be easy to find the symbol if it's here. It wasn't uncommon to bury treasure in fake graves back then so who knows, we could find something," Doogie said as he organized the small group.

They split up and walked among the headstones. Each person had approximately twenty-five stones to check. They bent over, squatted in the grass, tried to push broken ones back together and used their fingers to brush dirt away from the face of the stone to get a better visualization of the writing. When they finished, they returned to the main monument, each sadly shaking their head that they had found nothing.

"Let's not get discouraged," Megan said. "We don't know if there's treasure here and even if there is, there may not be a marker."

"You were right about the garbage," Doogie said. "It would take a few volunteers to clean this place up."

"Especially, the plastic," Georgie said as she teased Doogie.

"Well, it's true. Paper may eventually disintegrate, but the plastic will be here for a long time. At least it's not killing any sea life up here. I can't imagine it's good for birds or animals either."

"I guarantee I'll look into cleaning up the place and putting up a fence with a lock that will keep the high school kids out."

"What a bummer for the high school kids," Georgie said. "Drinking up here was almost a rite of passage."

"It's not safe up here, and the kids can drink on the beach like the rest of us did," Megan said sarcastically.

"Hey, you can see all of Misty Manor and the lighthouse from here," Amber said from the wall near the cliff overlooking the ocean. "I can see Tommy's car, so he must be with Billy now."

The rest of the gang walked over to the stone wall. "This must have been some pretty cool property in the early 1900's," Doogie said. "They were smart enough to know a home wouldn't be secure here, but what a great lookout."

Megan was quiet as she stared down at Misty Manor and the lighthouse.

"Hey, what's up?" Georgie asked as she looked at her friend. "You look like you've seen a ghost."

Megan shook her head. "Look at the back of the lighthouse. See that guy poking around down there?"

The group stared down for a minute. "Yes, I do see him," Georgie said. "Who is that?"

"Well, it's not Tommy," Amber said.

"I think that's Nathan Graham," Megan said. "I can't be one hundred percent sure from here, but it looks an awful lot like him."

"I'm calling Tommy," Amber said as she pulled out her cell phone and dialed. After a moment she hung up. "The reception up here stinks."

"I should call Nick as well," Megan said. "C'mon, let's get back in the car and go somewhere we can get through."

The group all piled into the car. Doogie drove as fast as he dared, Megan was eventually able to connect with Nick and hurriedly told him Nathan Graham was at the lighthouse. After speaking for a few minutes, she hung up. "Nick said he's on his way with other officers responding as well."

"I can't get hold of Tommy," Amber said worriedly. "He's not answering his phone, and he always answers his phone in case an agent is calling. He's not answering texts either."

"We're almost there," Doogie said as he careened around a corner. "Good thing I've got my jeep."

"As you can guess, Nick specifically said we should not go there and definitely not engage," Megan said.

"We can check it out," Amber said as she held on to the door handle. "We're not arresting the guy."

Doogie reached the end of Main Street and drove straight onto the beach. He stayed away from the water and crossed over the sand but had to slow down. As he reached the lighthouse, he threw the jeep in park, and the group jumped out.

The door of the lighthouse was standing open. "That's not right," Megan said. "Billy keeps that door closed, especially now that it's so difficult for him to walk down and close it."

"Tommy or Nathan must have left it open," Amber said.

"I'm not sure if that makes me feel better or worse," Georgie said.

"Stay in the car," Doogie said. "I'll go up to the door to see if anyone's nearby." He jumped out of the jeep and quickly crossed the sand to the lighthouse. He looked inside the door but jumped when Megan whispered near his ear.

"See anything?"

"What are you doing here? I said to stay in the car."

"Amber and Georgie are in the car, but I want to know what this son of a bitch is up to," Megan said as she leaned behind Doogie. "He almost killed me."

"Yeah, well, Nick will kill me if anything happens to you," Doogie said.

The two stopped talking when they heard yelling from above.

"Tell me where it is!"

Doogie advanced ten steps upward on the spiral staircase and craned his neck to see what was going on. After a few moments and more yelling, he went up another five steps and was able to see the floor of the landing above.

"I don't' know what the hell you're talking about," Tommy said as he stood with his hands held outward.

"Ask the old man. I want the treasure."

Doogie craned his neck upward and was able to make out the feet and legs of Nathan Graham holding a gun pointed at Tommy and Uncle Billy.

"What's going on?" Megan whispered. She had snuck up the stairs behind him. Doogie turned around and held his finger to his mouth.

"We don't know anything about a treasure," Tommy yelled. "You're nuts."

Megan jumped when she felt a hand at the small of her back. "Don't make any noise." She turned to find Nick standing right behind her. He grabbed her hand and slowly pulled her down the spiral staircase. When he finally had her to the entrance, he turned her around. "Get in that car and don't come out. We'll talk about this later."

Megan began to protest but stopped when she saw his face. He gestured and said, "Go." Megan trotted toward the jeep and jumped inside. When Nick turned around, Peters was pushing Doogie in the direction of the jeep as well. Then both men, with guns drawn, disappeared through the doorway of the lighthouse.

CHAPTER 43

"I've waited years to make a find like this," Graham yelled. "Studying all these Grand Victorian homes from the Gilded Age. I'm not leaving until I see the treasure."

Tommy was at a loss for words, but Billy yelled out. "Damn fool. Ain't nothing in here. Been living in here for years. If I knew about a treasure, I would've dug it up years ago."

"Shut up, old man," Nathan yelled.

"Go ahead and shoot. I ain't got more than a few years left anyhow. Tommy, move to the side of the door. The bastard probably couldn't find the trigger if he tried."

Nick and Officer Peters slowly crept up the stairs. Graham was standing at the door of the small lighthouse keeper apartment. Tommy stood inside the door, and Nick could see Billy sitting in a chair behind him.

Face red with rage, Nathan raised his arm.

"Stop, Police," Nick yelled as he ran up the last couple of steps. "Put the gun down."

"Stay back, Nick," Nathan said as he pivoted toward the stairway.

"Put the gun down," Nick directed once again. "We can talk about this."

"I'm done talking, Nick. I want to find the treasure."

"You're not making any sense," Nick said. "Put the gun down. Let's figure it out together. If we find treasure, you'll be able to see it. Killing someone isn't going to help anything."

"I could've killed Megan, but I didn't," Nathan said. "I don't want to hurt anyone, but I want the treasure."

"You hurt Wade. Why did you do that?" Nick yelled out.

Nathan took a deep breath. "I didn't mean to kill him. We met at the beach that night because he was supposed to help me break into the house. That was his specialty."

Nick felt more than heard Davis creep up the steps behind him. Peters continued to guard the base of the stairs.

"What happened?" Nick asked. "Why did you kill him?"

Nathan laughed as he shook his head in disbelief. "Can you believe after all those trips to jail, he finally found religion. Said he wasn't willing to help criminals anymore. He finally found a program to set him straight, and it started with the carpentry I taught him." Nathan laughed like a crazy man. "Can you believe that? He wasn't going to help me because I had helped him. What a crazy ass world."

"Put the gun down, Nathan, and tell me what happened," Nick said.

"Nothing to tell. Wade had the house under surveillance at night but then changed his mind and said he was going to tell Megan Stanford about the plan to steal the treasure map. Just like that. Pulled out at the last minute. We got into a fight. I couldn't let him talk to Megan."

"What did you do?" Nick continued to press.

"I punched him in the stomach and told him not to get up. I picked up one of the poles that hold up those beach tents. I held it against him and told him not to get up. We needed to sort it out. He hit the pole out of my hands, and it landed at an angle on the sand. Then he came at me. The two of us fought. At one point, he lunged at me, and I pulled to the side. The ass impaled himself right on the pole and dropped to the sand."

"We didn't find any pole near his body," Nick said.

"Of course not," Nathan laughed. "I knew my fingerprints were all over it, so I pulled it out of him and got rid of it."

"And you left him there to die?"

"His problem, stupid jerk."

"Enough, Nick," Davis whispered behind him. "Let's get him out of here."

"Put the gun down," Nick said again as he took another step closer to the landing. "We've got you covered. There's no way out." Nick looked at Tommy who had moved beyond the door. With a nod of his head, Tommy slammed the heavy wooden door to the apartment closed which left Nathan trapped on the spiral stairs.

"Don't come up here," Nathan screamed as he aimed a shot at the concrete wall. When Nick and Davis ducked for cover, Nathan turned and ran up the spiral stairs to the top of the lighthouse. The bullet ricocheted throughout the lower portion of the building and became lodged in a wooden board located in a storage area near the door.

Nick and Davis ran up the stairs to follow Graham while listening for the gun knowing a bullet could be just as dangerous if it ricocheted down the stairway. They listened as Nathan continued to pound up steps and they slowly followed him up as there was no way out.

Nathan reached the top of the stairs and looked around the metal landing. The door which opened to the stairs to the lantern room was locked, so Nathan was not able to go inside. Instead, he bolted into the service room and crouched in a corner. Looking around, he saw cleaning equipment and some tools.

He panted while he tried to catch his breath. His back was pushed up against the wall, his gun resting at his side. Turning his head to the side, he listened to their footfalls as they climbed the metal stairway behind him. Eventually, they reached the landing.

Nick tilted his head at the door to the lantern room while Davis covered him from the other side of the landing. He reached out for the door handle and realized it was locked which meant Nathan had either entered and locked the door behind him or was hiding in the service room. Once again, Nick gestured toward the door of the service room. The two men crept forward as Nick reached out for the wooden door. Before he could reach it, Nathan pushed the door open and threw a cup of liquid toward the men. Fumes immediately filled the small space as Nathan ran back into the service room. Nick and Davis retreated down to the next landing and tucked into the watch room. There was a small window that allowed some fresh air and both men pulled close to breathe it in.

"What the hell was that?" Davis asked as he waved his hand in front of his face.

"Smells like a mixture of ammonia and chlorine to me," Nick said as he breathed in fresh air.

"That stuff will kill your lungs," Davis said as the smell dissipated. They watched the stairway and as predicted Nathan tried to creep down the steps and go by them.

"Give it up, Graham. We're done playing here," Nick yelled as he ran toward the stairs.

Nathan saw him and retreated to the service room, where he bolted through a metal door and out onto the gallery deck. The platform circled the tower below the lantern room. Nathan ran to the far side and looked around for an escape.

Nick and Davis carefully entered the gallery deck. Through hand motions, they split up to circle the lighthouse and approach Nathan from both sides.

"Last chance, Graham. Give it up. There's nowhere to go from here," Nick yelled out.

Graham stood on the other side of the lighthouse, his back against the concrete wall. He twirled as he looked side to side. He smiled as he looked at the vast sea, the fluffy white clouds, the blue sky, and the jeep below. "Don't come around here, Nick. I don't want to shoot you."

"Throw the gun down and let's talk about it," Nick yelled out. "We're coming around."

Nathan was slightly turned toward Nick's direction when he heard a noise on the other side. He looked and saw Davis coming at him. Nathan raised the gun high and pulled off a shot. As Davis fell to the floor, Nathan jumped up and grabbed the metal ledge of the widow's walk above. Nick rushed toward them and tried to grab Nathan's legs, knowing he had to use both hands to pull himself upward. Without warning, the gun suddenly dropped and almost hit Nick in the head. He lost his grip for a moment while Nathan pulled another few inches upward and out of reach of Nick's hands. Kicking wildly, Nathan was almost at the rim of the widow's walk when a flock of birds flew toward the lighthouse. The seagulls startled Nathan as his hands slipped off the railing and he felt himself in a sudden free fall. He screamed out as his back hit the railing of the gallery deck and tipped him backward off the rail. He closed his eyes and hoped he wouldn't feel anything when his body hit the ground.

In the next few seconds, which felt like days to Nathan, Nick jumped up and grabbed Graham's leg. His hands contracted as the leg slipped through them and then finally latched around Nathan's boot.

Nick held the boot with two hands as Graham swung wildly, flailing his arms like windmills. As Nick was losing his grip, another pair of hands grabbed Graham's other leg. Peters had reached the gallery deck. Sweat dripping down his face, Nick took a deep breath as Peters reached down and grabbed Nathan Graham's pants and helped to stabilize him against the railing where Graham could clutch onto the metal.

Far below, Doogie and the women hopped out of the Jeep and looked up as they watched the fight unfold above them. Doogie herded the women away from the lighthouse for their safety and told them to close their eyes.

Nick hooked Nathan's boot over the railing and reached down and grabbed his belt. With one strong pull, he and Peters yanked Nathan up and over the railing and dropped him on the metal landing of the gallery walk. While gulping mouthfuls of air, Nick bent over and handcuffed Nathan to the railing. He then stood up and braced himself on the railing as he caught his breath and looked over at Davis.

Peters was kneeling by Davis. Nick ran over and squatted nearby. He began to check for a pulse by Davis's neck, but his hand was swatted away by the Captain. "Get off of me," Davis roared. "And someone better go watch your prisoner."

"Oh man, I thought you were dead," Nick said as Peters chuckled.

"Don't count me out yet," Davis said. "Save your celebration for another day."

"What the hell happened?" Nick said. "He fired a shot at you."

"Bullet hit my vest. I went down because I tried to jump out of the way and hit my head on the lighthouse concrete wall. Plus, a damned bullet hurts even with a vest. You breathe a word of that, and you're both fired."

"Are you okay?" Nick asked, containing a smirk.

"Bit of a headache, but I'll live," Davis said. "You're not getting rid of me that easily."

"That's fine, but you're going to the hospital to get checked out like everyone else," Nick said as he stood up and turned toward Peters.

"Thanks for jumping in. I was losing him." Peters nodded, pleased about the compliment. "Let's get this psycho out of here."

CHAPTER 44

"*A*re you okay?" Megan looked at Nick who had scratches on his face and neck. Davis had been loaded in a rig to go to the hospital. Nathan Graham was being driven to the police station by Peters and the three state troopers who showed up to assist. The rest of the crowd were all in the lighthouse keeper's apartment.

Nick stayed behind to get statements. He spoke at length to Tommy and Uncle Billy about their account of Nathan running up the circular steps, knocking on the door and demanding the treasure.

"I didn't know what he was asking for," Tommy said.

"Nothing," Uncle Billy spat. "Nothing but a stupid rumor."

Megan made her way over to the men. "I'm a little upset that you offered to put yourself in danger, Uncle Billy."

"Ahh, that guy was nuts," Billy said, waving his hand in a dismissive gesture. "He wouldn't know how to aim a gun if he had a laser focus."

"Still, you could've been shot or killed," Megan said, visibly upset.

"Ain't got nothing but pain on a daily basis anyway," Billy said. Megan frowned and made another resolution to help him, even if she had to start with a visiting physician. "I don't know what the hell he was going on about."

"He was talking about the treasure map," Tommy reminded him.

"I know that," Billy said, annoyance playing across his face. "He kept showing me the damned map, but there's no heads or tails about that map."

"I guess the map is gone now," Tommy said.

"Not necessarily," Nick said. "They'll take everything from his pockets, but if it's Megan's property, they'll eventually return it."

Megan pulled her phone out. "Billy, do you remember seeing anything like this?" She poked at her phone until she found the photo of the symbol. She turned the phone toward him so that he could see it better.

Billy stared at it for a while, then shook his head. "No, I ain't seen anything like that around here."

Tommy was looking over Billy's shoulder when Megan showed him the phone. "I've seen something like that. Ever since I was a little kid, but I didn't know it meant anything."

"Where? Where have you seen this?" Megan asked as she looked over toward Nick.

"Here, in the lighthouse. Downstairs near the big arches that make up the foundation of the lighthouse."

"The symbol is on the arches?" Megan's voice rose with excitement.

"No, it's actually near the floor, to the side of a door that opens on a floor vent." Tommy saw the confused look on Megan's face. "Do you remember playing in the lighthouse as a kid? You know those small wooden doors with a small arch that look like a teeny brick oven?"

Megan laughed. "Yes, I do. I used to ask if they were special rooms for mice. The arched wooden miniature doors built into the brick were adorable."

Tommy smiled. "Well, those little rooms are floor vents for the lighthouse. They serve to prevent moisture from building up in the lighthouse tower which is bad for the brick and ironwork in the building. The wooden doors are there to help control the air flowing from the vent up into the tower. The doors also help to keep dirt out of the vent when they're closed."

Megan was fascinated as Tommy described the features of the

hundred-year-old lighthouse. When she didn't respond, he continued, "Anyway, that symbol is inside one of those little vent rooms in the foundation of the building. I don't know why they call it a room. It's only a foot tall and wide," Tommy said. "More like a tiny alcove."

"I never saw any treasure downstairs," Billy said.

"I didn't say I saw a treasure," Tommy said. "I saw the symbol."

"Can you show us?" Megan asked before Billy could continue the argument.

"Sure, it's downstairs," Tommy said as he turned to go. The gang stood up and started to follow him, including Billy.

"Hey, wait for me. I want to see what you're up to."

Tommy slowed down and waited for his uncle to get to the stairs. Holding him by the crook of the arm, he helped him down the metal circular stairs as the rest of the gang followed behind. When they reached the bottom of the stairs, they walked forward through one of the large arches which made up the foundation of the lighthouse and helped to stabilize the tower. True to Tommy's word, they saw what looked like multiple wooden tiny round-topped doors near the floor. Tommy moved forward to the right and pointed to one of the doors.

"This one?" Megan asked pointing to the door.

"I'm pretty sure that's the one," Tommy said. "You have to open it."

Megan dropped to the floor and opened the tiny door and looked inside. In the back of the small alcove, there was a grate which covered a vent leading into the building. Megan could feel cool air flowing toward her from the vent. "Now what?"

"Look to the left, and you'll see the symbol on the wall," Tommy said.

Nick tucked in close to Megan and pulled the flashlight off his police belt. He turned it on and pointed it toward the brick wall. Both were surprised when they saw the symbol immediately appear.

"I see it," Megan said excitedly.

"So, do I," Nick said nearby.

"Okay, then we've all seen it. What does it mean?" Tommy asked while the group stood behind him and watched Megan and Nick explore.

Megan reached out and pressed the brick near the symbol. She covered most of the small wall before she came to a cinderblock which was slightly loose. "Nick, this one is moving, but I can't grasp it."

"Let me try," he said as he changed positions with her. "Hold this." Nick handed her the flashlight and then knelt. He leaned forward and grasped the cinderblock. He pushed and shifted until he was able to slide the front of the cinderblock out of its space. The face of the cinderblock hid a cavity where the rest of the original cinderblock should be. Nick took the flashlight back from Megan and directed it into the cavity. "Holy smokes," he said as he shook his head.

"Let me see," Megan said as she pushed forward. "Did we find it?"

Nick handed her the flashlight, and she peered inside. "Oh, my Lord," Megan said. She grabbed her phone and immediately took photos. Then leaning forward, she reached inside and took out a small treasure chest matching the one at Misty Manor.

The gang was quiet behind her until they suddenly burst out with sound. Megan heard various shouts, "Open it up," or "Let me see," and "Can you believe it?"

She placed the small treasure chest on the floor and stared at it. "Nick, my hands are shaking. I'm afraid to open it."

"We went through all this, you've got to get it over with, but wait until I get my phone, so we can record it in case Teddy gets upset."

Megan waited until Nick was recording and slowly opened the treasure chest as the group moved in behind her. The first thing she withdrew was a shell. It was a beautifully polished conch shell around six inches long. Next was a sand dollar, some dried flowers, which was followed by beautiful sea glass. She then found a small antique metal compass, spyglass and gold coins. As she dug deeper, she found a small strand of pearls and under the pearls, she found a photo. When she pulled it out, she wasn't quite sure who was pictured.

"Hey, let me see that," Billy quipped from behind her. Megan handed the photo to Billy who held it close to his eyes. He then smiled, and a small tear dropped on his cheek. "That's George." Billy was excited as he held the photo up for others to see from afar. "This is a photo of George when he was a young boy. Megan, that's your great-grandparents standing behind him, and I think the pearls in the treasure chest are the ones Mary is wearing in the picture."

The last thing in the chest was a letter written by John Stanford. Megan handed it to Nick who read aloud.

Matthew 6:21
For where your treasure is, there your heart will be also –

OF ALL THE treasures I've seen in the world, on all my travels, there are none more precious to me than the love of my wife, Mary, and my son, George. We place these special things in this chest in remembrance of our love, unity, and bond while on this earth and into the next. Whether through body or soul we shall be linked always through eternity, never to be torn asunder.

John Anthony Stanford
Mary Elizabeth Stanford
George Albert Stanford

NICK HANDED the letter to Megan who was sobbing. He dropped down next to her and hugged her. "What's wrong? We finally found the treasure."

"I know," Megan whispered. "It's so sad. The treasure was a special family remembrance when George was a young boy. They probably missed each other so much when he went out to sea, the family made a treasure bond. Imagine how devastated John and Mary must have been when George disappeared years later. No wonder John never went back to the secret room. His treasure had nothing to do with beautiful things, but rather what he valued in life, which was true unconditional love. Being lucky enough to find that in life is truly a treasure indeed."

Nick hugged Megan to his chest and stroked her hair as he slowly placed each item back into the small treasure chest and replaced it in the wall where the bond of a family belonged, undisturbed, forever.

CHAPTER 45

$\mathcal{M}$egan stretched before she threw the ball toward the ocean for Dudley. He flew to the edge of the water, grabbed the ball and ran back to deliver his prize. She scratched him behind the ears, bent down, kissed his head and threw the ball again.

Turning around, she checked to see how Nick was doing with the barbecue they set up on the beach. He was busy grilling burgers, hot dogs, chicken and ribs for the gang, who were sharing a great beach day.

He watched as she walked up to him. He kissed her on the cheek and whispered in her ear, "Mustard or ketchup." She laughed and punched him in the shoulder as she grabbed cold beers from the cooler and passed them to her friends.

"Thank you," Georgie said as she tipped her bottle toward Megan.

"Only a wine cooler for me," Amber said as she adjusted her swim outfit. Rolling her eyes, Megan reached back into the cooler and pulled out a peach wine cooler for Amber.

"Tommy? Would you like a beer?"

Tommy paused. "Okay, but only one. I want to be on point at the concert tonight."

"You got it," Megan said as she turned and walked over to Doogie.

She held a beer out for him. He nodded his thanks as he took the bottle and toasted her. "Thanks again for everything you've done for me and our cause. We've gotten enough donations to purchase the sand rake, get rid of plastic on the beach and place other receptacles for recycling."

"I've got to say, that was a brilliant idea," Nick added as he walked over with a platter of food. "Tell us how you did it again."

Megan chuckled and shrugged. "I planted the idea in the right places the true treasure of Misty Point was our beach and our community, which is why we should all come together to keep it as clean as possible. Ed, my old boss at the Virtual News in Detroit, helped me publish an article about how the real treasure in Misty Point is the natural beauty of the beach."

"And you managed to turn that whole viral concept into an environmental public service announcement on protecting the beach and earth's natural beauty," Tommy said as he bit into a hot dog. "When you get a chance, I'd love for you to work on some marketing for the band."

"Oh, stop," Megan said, dismissing him with a wave.

"When will the cemetery be done?" Amber said.

"In a couple of weeks. I hired someone to reset the stones, remove all the garbage, and maintain the grass and weeds," Megan said as she sipped her beer. "I think Davenport was disappointed the project came together so quickly. Once we went to the high school and explained we needed help for a community project, a lot of people joined us for the cleanup."

"It's a special place for the high school kids. They appreciate it being as clean as the rest of the town."

Doogie walked over and snagged a burger from the platter. "And the library?"

"That's the best part," Megan said. "I spoke with the board, and they agreed to start a historical compendium about Misty Point, Misty Manor, and the Stanford family. We'll include stories about many of the townspeople and their good works. That way, the town history will be recorded somewhere official forever and always."

"That's great. Who knows who'll be reading it one hundred years from now?" Nick said as he put the empty platter on the table.

"Well, when they do, they'll read about a very special group of friends who loved and supported each other, forever. Thank you for always being there. You are my greatest treasure, and I love you guys." Megan held up her beer to toast her friends as they stood together in a bond of friendship. "We'll always be together." Megan took a sip of her drink and said, "To the next adventure.

AUTHOR'S NOTE

If you are interested in more information on shipwrecks in NJ, I would recommend you visit the NJ Maritime Museum.

njmaritimemuseum.org

NJ Maritime Museum
528 Dock Road, Beach Haven, NJ 08008
609-492-0202
info@njmaritimemuseum.org

The New Jersey Maritime Museum is located in Beach Haven on the southern end of Long Beach Island. You can visit them to explore the most extensive collection of maritime history and artifacts in the state of New Jersey.

ABOUT THE AUTHOR

Linda Rawlins is an American writer of mystery fiction best known for her Misty Point Mystery Series. She is also the author of the Rocky Meadow Mysteries including The Bench, Fatal Breach and Sacred Gold. She loved to read as a child and started writing her first mystery novel in fifth grade. She then went on to study science, medicine and literature, eventually graduating medical school and establishing her career in medicine.

Linda Rawlins lives in New Jersey with her husband, her family and spoiled pets. She loves spending time at the beach as well as visiting the mountains of Vermont. She is an active member of Mystery Writers of America as well as the 2018 Central Jersey VP of Sisters in Crime.

Visit Linda at lindarawlins.com and sign up for her mailing list to be the first to know about new releases, appearances, and more.

facebook.com/lindarawlinsauthor

twitter.com/lrl8

instagram.com/lindarawlins

ALSO BY LINDA RAWLINS

The Misty Point Mystery Series

Misty Manor

Misty Point

Misty Winter

The Rocky Meadow Mystery Series

The Bench

Fatal Breach

Sacred Gold

Made in the USA
Middletown, DE
09 February 2019